W9-BYS-117

ALSO BY
LISI HARRISON

The Clique series
The Alphas series
The Girl Stuff series
The Pack series

FOR OLDER READERS

The Monster High series
The Pretenders series

THE PACK #2

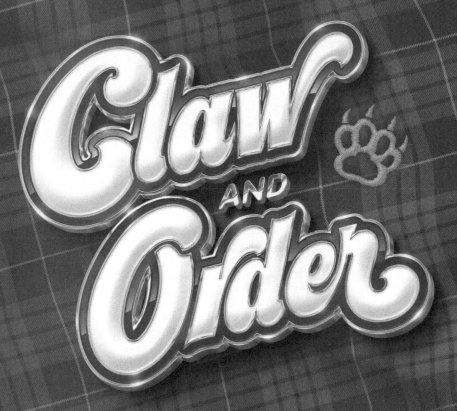

Claw
AND
Order

LISI HARRISON

DELACORTE PRESS

Text copyright © 2022 by Lisi Harrison
Jacket art copyright © 2022 by Luke Lucas

All rights reserved. Published in the United States by Delacorte Press, an imprint of Random House Children's Books, a division of Penguin Random House LLC, New York.

Delacorte Press is a registered trademark and the colophon is a trademark of Penguin Random House LLC.

Visit us on the Web! rhcbooks.com

Educators and librarians, for a variety of teaching tools, visit us at RHTeachersLibrarians.com

Library of Congress Cataloging-in-Publication Data is available upon request.
ISBN 978-0-593-18073-0 (hardcover) — ISBN 978-0-593-18074-7 (ebook)

The text of this book is set in 12.5-point Adobe Garamond Pro.
Interior design by Carol Ly

Printed in the United States of America
10 9 8 7 6 5 4 3 2 1
First Edition

For my brother-in-law, Marc Cooper.
Writing this novel while grieving destroyed me.
Writing this novel while grieving saved me.
Like the characters in the pages that follow,
you were a rare and special light.

one

*T*he classroom smelled like a Sephora. Instead of paying attention to Professor Norma's snoozer of a lecture on landforms, the caged animal-lights were swiping fruit-flavored gloss across their lips and rubbing floral-scented salves into their hands—all in anticipation of that final gong. Once struck, Typical Topics would be over, and the most anticipated weekend of the year (since last month's dance with the Allendale boys) would finally begin.

Sadie gazed beyond the metal-framed windows. Those smoke-gray clouds were still hovering. Oppressive and suffocating, they loomed above the private grounds of the Charm House boarding school like an overbearing parent, there to put a damper on her plans and, even worse, her new hairstyle. Hair that Sadie spent most of the day admiring in the reflection of her dead laptop screen.

She'd meant to charge her computer the night before. Really. But Claw Spa, the new beauty salon Sadie was opening with her pack mates, had become a major attention suck.

Saturday morning was fully booked, and they were wildly unprepared.

Lindsey, tiger-light and queen of the claws, had to set up a manicure table. Taylor, chameleon-light and color expert, needed a dyeing station. Amy, snake-light and scaly skin specialist, had to blend her oil treatments. And Sadie, lion-light with superhuman strength and a dry blond mane, was stuck rearranging furniture—a bummer, but not a surprise.

They had finished setting up around midnight. While Lindsey, Taylor, and Amy applauded their work, Sadie, now surrounded by mirrors, fixated on her unruly hair. Gathering it in a bristly bundle, she tried twisting it into something elegant at the nape of her neck. Tying straw into a bow would have been easier. "I should just shave it off."

"Funny," Taylor said as she worked her short pink layers into spikes. "I've been thinking about all of that"—she waved her hand in the general vicinity of Sadie's head—"and I have an idea. Trust me."

"You've been *thinking* about it?" How long had Taylor been contemplating Sadie's look? "Is it *that* bad?" Her stomach dipped as she remembered the girls at her old school, how they called her Hairy Poppins. And Taylor's whole "trust me" thing? That was an elephant-sized ask.

Only weeks earlier, Taylor had secretly terrorized the animal-lights—and worse, her own pack mates. Her plan was to scare the girls (mostly Lindsey) so they would stop sneaking out to meet the boys. If the animal-lights were discovered, the evil doctors at Institute of Behavioral Science would lock them in cages on the thirteenth floor, just like they did with Kate, and experiment on them 24/7. So Taylor's intention was to keep them safe. *But really, T? Did you have to turn invisible, scratch venom into our bodies to make us sleep, then carve the number 13 into our skin? You couldn't think of any other way to keep us safe from IBS? Nothing?*

Apparently, she couldn't. And technically, that was fine. Taylor meant well and the Pack forgave her. But "trust"? Yeah, that was going to take a while.

"Sadie, I'm not saying your frizzy vibe is *brutal*," she continued. "I'm just—"

"Then I'll say it," Lindsey interrupted, her emerald-green eyes fierce and focused. "Sadie Lady, we love you, but your frizzy vibe is brutal."

"*Brutal* is a little harsh," Amy said. "*Brittle* is more appropriate." Her sympathetic smile revealed one fang on either side of her mouth. "Why don't I heat some orange and clove oil and—"

"We can give you a mane-over!" Taylor bellowed.

"Purrrfect," Lindsey said. "I'll do her claws!"

Two hours later, Sadie was running the sharp points of her gold nails through flat-ironed, deep-conditioned blond hair that faded to black.

"Wow, you look sixteen!" Amy gushed.

"Yeah, the ombré technique is a total mane-changer," Taylor said. "And the dark tips hide your split ends."

"You actually look pretty!" Lindsey added.

"Actually?"

"Not that you didn't look pretty before. You did. On the inside. But now you're pretty on the outside, too."

Sadie was too excited about her mane-over to be offended. Before heading to bed, Taylor gave her a bottle of dry shampoo and strict instructions not to get her hair wet or it would frizz again. Which was why Sadie was currently admiring her reflection in a dead laptop screen and praying the rain away instead of listening to—

"Miss Samson!" Professor Norma shouted, or maybe it just sounded like a shout because of Sadie's extra-sensitive hearing. "Are you paying attention?"

Chairs creaked as everyone turned.

"Uh . . ." Sadie's cheeks warmed. "You were talking about animal migration."

"Correct. I *was* talking about animal migration. Twenty minutes ago . . ."

The hyena-lights giggled. Jealous of the Pack's popularity, they feasted on their misfortunes.

"Now I'm asking our Charm Club leaders for status reports, and since you're one of those leaders, why don't you update us on your progress."

Lindsey, Taylor, and Amy glared at Sadie, silently reminding her not to divulge their secret. As if she needed a reminder. The Charm Club project was worth 50 percent of their Typical Topics grade. And with her slipping GPA, Sadie was counting on a high score to bring up her average. If word got out that their club, the Claw Spa, was charging for treatments, they'd fail. Granted, the Pack wasn't asking for money. Just that customers cover the Pack's chores and hand over their desserts whenever asked. This seemed like a reasonable request, considering Claw Spa was the only club providing an essential service. But try telling that to a professor preaching a free-flowing exchange of ideas and teamwork.

"Our progress?" Sadie lowered the screen on her laptop. "Um, last night we set up the spa in our dorm rooms, and it opens tomorrow. That's about it."

Professor Norma lowered her glasses, which were attached to a beaded string that held them around her neck, against her navy cardigan. Her small features were tight, and her makeup-free skin was the color of Silly Putty. She was probably a terrible joke-teller. "Can you share your most positive experience so far?"

Sadie reached for the glossy tips of her hair and sat up a little taller. "Um, the Allendale football game is tomorrow night, and Family Day is Sunday, so we're booked solid, which is cool."

"Sounds promising." The professor searched Sadie's eyes like hiding places. "And your most challenging experience?"

"Fitting everyone in, I guess. Demand is pretty high."

"Well, you are offering a *free* service."

"Free?" Val yipped. "Ha!" She and the other hyena-lights had started a comedy club named Cackle. Ever since Professor Norma had said she thought the name was clever (*cackle* is the sound of a laugh, and it's also the name for a group of hyenas), Val had been incredibly cocky.

Professor Norma folded her arms across her dangling glasses. "Is there a problem?"

"Only if you think doing someone else's chores is a—"

Lindsey growled softly.

"Chores?" Professor Norma's thin eyebrows arched.

Lindsey glowered at Val and whispered, "Watch it, hy-e-nerd," knowing that Professor Norma couldn't hear her.

"Val, are you suggesting that—"

"Nope. All good. I was just workshopping one of my jokes for the Family Day showcase. I guess it needs more work. Sorry about that."

Unlike the other teachers at Charm House, Professor "Normal" did not have an animal-light, so quiet whispers often went undetected. Sadie often wondered why Headmistress Flora had hired a Typical in the first place. Yes, she taught Typical Topics, so that part made sense, but still. The whole point of Charm House was to protect its students from the outside world. A world in which researchers from the Institute of Behavioral Science hunted animal-lights and imprisoned them on the thirteenth floor of their creepy building, where they experimented on their prisoners and would continue to do so until the source of their animal powers was uncovered. Professor Norma's daughter was a light, which was why everyone trusted her. But what kind of light? And where was this daughter? Was she with Kate—Amy's old roommate, who had been captured by IBS the week before Sadie arrived? No one seemed to know.

"Who else will be presenting their club during the Family Day showcase?" the professor asked.

Before anyone could answer, the gong rang. The weekend had officially started, and the students began clearing out.

"Miss Samson, may I have a few words?"

"Of course." Smiling, Sadie made her way to the front of the room, anticipating another compliment. All her other teachers had had something positive to say about her hair, and every student (except the hyena-lights, of course) had booked a spa appointment, hoping for a similar look. If Professor Normal's few words were flattering, she could have as many as she wanted.

"I've noticed a change in you lately," she said once Sadie approached her desk.

"I elevated my style."

Professor Normal glanced at Sadie's black tips. "I see that."

An awkward silence filled the space between them. A

space that no longer smelled like fruity gloss and floral salves. Just tension.

"Any chance of you elevating your grades?"

"My *grades*?" Was *that* was this was about? Because come on. For the first time, Sadie had best friends, regular friends, and a crush on an Allendale boy who liked her back. As the only lion-light at Charm House, she no longer feared mean girls; they feared *her*. She was CEO of Claw Spa. Boss-lady of the jungle. Leader of the Pack. Yes, socializing had been cutting into her study time lately. But she'd bounce back. Good grades had always come easy to her. But BFFs? Not as much.

"I'm concerned," Professor Normal said with a coffee-scented sigh. "The other teachers are, too."

"Don't worry. I'm a cat. We always land on our feet."

"Do you think your parents will feel the same way?"

"I do," Sadie said, sure of it. Her parents always wanted her to branch out and make friends. So yeah, they would feel the same way. How could they not?

two

The Claw Spa opened its dorm-room doors immediately after breakfast, and now Sadie's bacon-free belly was shouting, *Time for lunch!* Had it been five hours already? She chased her hunger with cucumber-infused water, then greeted her next customer.

"Welcome to Claw Spa," she said to Sondra, a petite rat-light with chin zits and oily brown hair. "Checking in?"

Sondra nodded, brows raised, smile wide. Like a caterpillar on the verge of metamorphosis, she, and the dozens who checked in before her, wanted a beauty transformation, just like Sadie's. "I'm getting ombré hair with Taylor and an oil treatment with Amy."

"Same," said her friend Kara—a dingo-light with deep-set brown eyes and sharp, uneven teeth. "Can you see if Lindsey has time to do my nails?"

Sadie checked her spreadsheet. "I can squeeze you in with Lindsey if Sondra skips her treatment with Amy."

Did it make sense? No. Amy's schedule had nothing to do

with Lindsey's. But someone had to stop Sondra from getting an oil treatment, or her already greasy hair would look wet.

"What do you say?" Sadie asked, desperate to speed things up. The check-in line was snaking into the hallway, and the reception area was standing room only. The beds, which Sadie converted into couches thanks to some creative pillow placement, were taken. Same with the four chairs she positioned under Amy's heat lamp. Who knew the hot orange light, meant for warming cold-blooded reptiles, could cut nail-polish drying time in half? Lindsey, that's who.

Sondra approved the change, and Kara thanked her with a suffocating hug.

"Once you agree to the terms, you'll be all set." Sadie folded a piece of paper and slid it across her desk. It read: *Kara and Sondra do our laundry Monday, November 8.* Then she handed them a pen. "Your signatures, please."

They scribbled their names without hesitation, and Sadie filed the paper away in her desk drawer. "Next!"

Rachel stepped forward. An energetic monkey-light with a nasty nail-biting habit and the swollen cuticles to prove it. "One manicure, please."

"What about a hot oil hand massage?" Sadie said, realizing that Sondra's cancellation left Amy wide open. "Those cuticles look parched." If Rachel's bloody nubs came within five feet of Lindsey, she'd pack up her Caboodles kit and walk off the job.

"But I booked a manicure."

"Yeah, but right now, you need a little less mani and a lot more *cure*. The oil treatment will be perfect."

Rachel began nibbling on her thumbnail.

"Trust me." Sadie slid a folded piece of paper across her desk, which Rachel promptly signed. Now that Sadie had someone to return the water glasses to the cafeteria after closing, she could dry-shampoo her hair, raid Lindsey's closet for a flattering outfit, and get to Allendale without missing a second of the football game.

Not that Sadie liked football. She loathed it. Her father, a San Francisco superfan, always shouted at the TV when the 49ers played. Which, thanks to Sadie's super-sensitive lion-light hearing, sounded like he was screaming into a megaphone aimed at a microphone.

It was Beak she looked forward to—a like-minded sports hater who also preferred books to balls. And she hadn't seen him, or his distracting green eyes, since the dance, four weeks earlier. She listened to "Without Me" by Halsey several times a day to relive their magical night.

Beak's warm breath against her neck while they swayed to the heart-pounding beat of the song. The grape bubble gum scent of his skin. How the twinkle lights in the gym hinted at the C-shaped scar on his cheek—a scar he got while breaking up a fight between his sister and an innocent girl at a coffee shop. How he shared his most guarded secret—that this sister was Lindsey—and Lindsey had no idea that Beak was her brother. . . .

Granted, Beak already knew that Miss Flora (his grandmother) and Professor Jo (his mother) had let Sadie in on the family secret. What choice did they have? Sadie figured it out. But Beak said he was relieved that he had someone to talk to about it and that that someone was Sadie. Which made the soda-pop love mist inside Sadie's belly fizz even more.

Since then, they'd texted frequently and shared each other's locations on Trkr. She loved seeing a picture of his face move around the app's map as he roamed the Allendale campus, loved knowing where he was. Not because she was a stalker, but because it helped her feel connected to Beak when they were apart. There hadn't been any more school-approved occasions for the Charm House girls to hang out with the Allendale boys until this football game. And Sadie couldn't wait! She'd put in her earplugs, cozy up to Beak on the bleachers, share her popcorn, and captivate him with her new hair. Then, as if hearing her thoughts, he texted.

BEAK

> I have a surprise. R U def going
> to the game tonight?

Sadie started sending the first part of her message, then got distracted by a vicious-sounding growl from the salon. She dashed next door to find Lindsey circling Val and Liv in the hallway—claws drawn, ready to pounce.

Taylor and Amy, both reptile-lights, didn't have the strength to pull a tiger away from two hyenas, but they had the smarts.

While Amy hissed warnings and gnashed her venomous fangs, Taylor, now invisible, was tying their shoelaces together.

"What's going on?" Sadie asked. Her voice was deep and commanding as if to say: *My hair may be pretty, but I'm tough.*

Lindsey lowered her claws. Another cat had arrived. She could relax. "These hyea*nerds* need to leave; that's what's going on."

"Speciest!" Val said.

"Come here and say that so I can scratch the freckles off that tragic face of yours." Lindsey lifted her gold nail file necklace, twisting the chain around her finger.

Val saw red when anyone made fun of her freckles and she lunged toward Lindsey. Not realizing that Taylor had tied her and Val's laces together, Liv jerked forward, smashed into Val, and they toppled to the floor.

Hilarious as it was, the Pack knew better than to waste this moment on a laugh. They were standing above their prey—the ultimate power position. They needed to stay serious.

Liv snarled, her thin lips quivering with conviction. "You can't turn us away because we're hyenas."

"We're not," Taylor began. "We're turning you away because—"

Lindsey held her palm in front of Taylor's face. *I've got this.* "For one, you need an appointment. For two, you don't have one. And for three, you never will."

"Why?" Val asked as she struggled to separate her laces from Liv's.

"For one, you didn't make an appointment," Sadie said.

"And for two—" Taylor said.

"You tried to rat us out in class yesterday," Lindsey said, interrupting Taylor again.

"I take offense to that!" Sondra, the rat-light, called from the reception area.

"You should."

"You can't refuse a paying customer," Liv insisted.

"You're not a paying customer," Sadie said. "You're literally refusing to pay."

"Because you're not supposed to be charging!"

Just then, Mia, a hyena-light and the third member of

14

Cackle, showed up. Or maybe she had been there the whole time. Petite and shy, Mia wasn't outspoken like Val and Liv and was often overlooked when they were around. She didn't try to make a joke out of everything, and she had never picked a fight with the Pack. Her full-moon face was welcoming, her warm brown eyes and heavy lids patient. She was attractive but not in a threatening way. Not like Lindsey. Mia's beauty was understated and kind. If it had a profession, it would probably be a nurse.

"We should head over to the barn," Mia said, flashing her clipboard. "We only have the stage for thirty minutes, and we need to rehearse our blocking."

Val and Mia finally stood.

"Blocking? For what?" Amy asked like someone who cared.

"Cackle," Mia offered. "We're performing for the Family Day showcase tomorrow and—"

Val shot her a silencing glare. "Which is *why* we want our nails done."

"Which is *why* you need an appointment," Sadie snapped.

"But we can't get an appointment unless we do your stupid chor—"

Sadie cut her off with a growl.

Lindsey aimed her gold nail file at Val's face and *scrape-scrape-scraped* the air. "Say one more thing about the chores, and I'll be tossing your freckles like confetti at tonight's football game."

"If Professor Normal finds out you're doing this, she's going to fail you," Liv said, swiping lip balm across those thin, chapped lips of hers.

Sadie stepped closer. "Professor Normal is not going to find out, IS SHE?"

"Pack huddle," Taylor said. Once their foreheads were pressed together, she whispered, "Maybe we should give them appointments. You know, so they don't tell."

"That's your *solution*?" Lindsey roared. "We give in?" She broke away from the huddle and hurried back to her room. "I have *paying* customers to see." Lindsey held up her gold nail file like a middle finger, strode into the Claw Spa, and slammed the door behind her.

"Let's go," Mia told Val and Liv. "We need to get to the barn." Then, *ding*.

As the hyenas loped away, Sadie checked her phone. *Beak!*

BEAK

U got something against surprises?

Confused, Sadie reread their earlier messages, and her stomach lurched. She had been in the middle of writing *Can't wait*, meaning, "I can't wait for your surprise." But then Lindsey had growled, she'd gotten distracted, and all she'd sent was the word *Can't*.

Ha! SRRY. Meant to say,
"Can't wait for the game. and
the surprise." BTW what is it?

BEAK

Doesn't matter.
Game is canceled.

SADIE

Why????

BEAK

Look outside.

Sadie returned to her room, pushed past the girls by the reception desk, and hurried toward the window. The sky was elephant gray and the rain was coming down sideways. Now that the Allendale game was canceled, everyone wanted to move their appointments.

"But Family Day is tomorrow," Sadie pleaded. "Don't you want to look good for your parents?"

Heads shook.

With a gusty sigh, Sadie returned to her computer and began changing the schedule. Amidst the chaos, she palmed the back of her head to make sure her hair was still smooth. It was. At least there was that.

Exhausted from hours spent rescheduling appointments and rearranging dorm-room furniture, Sadie considered using her dinner plate as a pillow but took five pieces of bacon instead and gobbled them down before Ms. Finkle noticed. The owl-light roamed the caf enforcing proper table manners, and the last thing Sadie needed now was detention for "eating like an animal."

"I can't believe everyone canceled," Amy said with a shiver. The tunnel-shaped dining hall was extra chilly because of the storm, and the cold-bloods were miserable. "I get wanting to look good for the Allendale game, but what about Family Day?" She wrapped her hands around a steaming mug of hot chocolate. "What about our parents?"

"What *about* them?" Lindsey asked, her gaze lifting to the stained-glass windows, where the rain beat down against the panes as if to torture those with sensitive hearing. She and Sadie had stuffed napkins in their ears. It still sounded like bullets on a tin roof.

"I can't wait to see Lori and Dean," Sadie said. "And I *really* can't wait for them to see *me*." The hair, the nails, the friends. Sadie was nothing like the daughter they'd left at Charm House six weeks earlier. She had found her pack.

"My parents probably won't see me at all," Taylor mumbled, mindlessly moving salad around her plate. "Last Family Day, Nick and Elizabeth were on their phones the whole time, quote, 'closing deals and putting out fires,' end quote. I spent half the day in camo-mode watching dance videos on YouTube. They didn't even notice."

"Football game or not, I still want to look good for Joe and Meg," Amy said.

"You should start by washing *that*." Lindsey indicated the mess of black hair on Amy's head. What was once an elegant topknot had downgraded into something more like tumbleweed.

"Trust me. I'm going to do it all. I want them to be proud of me for more than the whole straight-As thing."

Lindsey coughed, *"Humblebrag."*

Amy coughed back, *"Jealousmuch?"*

Taylor shot Amy an *I-can't-believe-you-just-said-that* look.

Amy lifted the mug to her lips. "What?" she asked. "What's wrong with saying jealousmu—" She lurched forward. Hot chocolate splashed all over her white fleece jacket. "What the heck, Tay? Why'd you kick me?"

"I *didn't*," Taylor insisted, her hazel eyes wide in a *go-with-it* sort of way.

"Yes, you—" Amy began. Then, "Oh." She lowered her mug and her eyes. "Sorry, Linds. I meant jealous of my grades, not my parents. I mean—"

"Um, hello, I'm fine," Lindsey managed. Then to Taylor, "Just because I don't have parents doesn't mean you can't. Stop worrying about me. I don't even care."

But Lindsey did care, and she did have a family. Headmistress Flora was her grandmother. Professor Jo was her mother. Beak was her brother. And the evil man behind IBS's animal-light cruelty was Karl Van der Beak—her father. She just didn't know it. Convincing Lindsey that she was alone in the world was the best way to tame her restless spirit and keep her at Charm House. The best way to keep her safe and prevent her father from discovering her powers. And all Sadie could do was play dumb and watch her friend suffer.

"So now I'm wrong for being a good friend?" Taylor's bright orange sweatshirt turned granite gray, matching the stone walls behind her.

"What's that supposed to mean?"

"It means you never agree with anything I say."

"That's not true."

"See?"

Suddenly, a wrinkled hand clamped down on Taylor's granite-colored shoulder. "No camouflaging during meals," Ms. Finkle said. Amber eyes aglow, she stood there waiting for Taylor to shift back.

"It's hard to do when you're watching me," Taylor said.

"You have three minutes," Ms. Finkle said, her Crocs

squeaking against the polished floors as she backed away. "Two-fifty-nine, two fifty-eight, two fifty-seven . . ."

"Okay," Taylor said as her sweatshirt slowly returned to orange.

"That woman is the *owl* in *scowl,*" Amy said with a shudder.

Everyone laughed except Lindsey, who took a bite of her double cheeseburger, tossed the rest onto her plate, then pushed the tray aside. The gold bangles on her wrist clanged.

"Fine, yes. It sucks that I don't know who my parents are. So forgive me for not caring how I look on Family Day, okay?"

Which was kind of a funny-not-funny thing to say, considering Lindsey never had to care. Natural beauties with supernatural style rarely did. Her butterscotch-blond hair was streaked with black tiger stripes. Her emerald-green eyes were hypnotic. And her gait was mesmerizing; Lindsey didn't walk; she padded. How someone so mighty, so athletic, could move as if weightless was a real mane-scratcher.

"There, Taylor, I admitted it sucks. Happy?" Before Taylor could respond, Lindsey added, "Miss Flora's memory elixir doesn't work. Never has, never will." She pulled a vial from her pocket and emptied it over her burger. "I don't know why I bother."

Sadie grabbed Lindsey by the wrist, hoping to salvage a few drops. "What are you doing? You need that!"

"Um, hello, no, I don't. I've been taking it for years, and I still don't remember anything from my past."

Of course she didn't. Her grandmother (Headmistress Flora) and her mother (Professor Jo) gave her daily micro-doses of Amy's snake venom to make her *forget* life before Charm House. They believed they had to, that it was the only way to keep Lindsey safe. But did that make it right?

They had to do something. Lindsey hated being cooped up at Charm House and wanted to live in the Typicals' world. *Our animal light should be celebrated, not hidden,* she often said. And that was true. Not that "true" mattered.

"It's official," Sadie announced. "You're spending Family Day with Lori and Dean."

The scent of roses and leather filled the air—the unmistakable smell of pride. "I'm good," Lindsey said. "I'm going to sneak over to Allendale and hang with Link."

The girls exchanged a look of concern. Sneaking out of Charm House was a major offense. If one girl got caught, they'd all lose their football game privileges.

"You can't!" Taylor snapped.

"Don't worry. No one will know."

"What if you get attacked by IBS again," she said, alluding to the recent incident where Lindsey, Amy, and Beak had all been found unconscious with the number 13 scratched into their skin—a warning that they could end up on the thirteenth floor of IBS, never to be seen again.

"Tay," Lindsey snickered. "The attacker wasn't from IBS. You know that, right?"

"How can you be sure?"

Lindsey's brows shot up. "Because it was *you*, trying to scare us so we'd stop sneaking out!"

"Well, it didn't work. So I might have to try something else. Something *worse*."

"I'll know it's you, so I won't be scared."

Taylor giggled. "Valid."

"No one is sneaking out," Sadie insisted. "Lindsey, you're hanging with the Samsons tomorrow. I insist."

Lindsey's tight expression softened. "Thanks, Sadie Lady, but I don't want your pity."

"It's not pity. It's Family Day, and we're family now . . ." Emotion expanded inside Sadie's chest, making it hard to get the words out. "Lori and Dean are going to love you as much as I do. I promise," she said. "What's not to love?"

three

High-pitched greetings pierced the midmorning air as families reunited on the back lawn of Charm House. The breeze was full of wet bark and leaf smells. And the sun, having decided that Family Day was more important than last night's Allendale football game, beamed like a proud parent. But not Sadie's mom. She was all gloom.

Her orangey-brown eyes lacked their usual glimmer, and her curls hung limp. Dean may or may not have felt the same. It was impossible to know. He was just staring, his expression like the anguished face emoji—brows high, eyes wide, mouth agape.

"I hate it," Lori said as she released her daughter from a lavender-scented hug. A hug that, only weeks earlier, would have made Sadie weepy and homesick. But not anymore. Sadie was already home.

" 'Hate' is a strong word."

"And that is a strong hairstyle."

Sadie rolled her eyes. "It's not a hairstyle, Mom. It's ombré."

"It's *something*, that's for sure." Lori looked to her ex-husband for backup, but he was "busy" eyeing the pastry selection. Classic Dean. Anything to stay out of a mother-daughter flare-up.

"I thought you were all about individual expression, Mom."

Lori evaluated the crowd. "I am, though there's nothing *individual* about your expression. At least five other girls have the same questionable taste as you."

"I know!" Sadie boasted. "They copied me." She turned to Lindsey, who was standing silently by her side. "Didn't they, Linds?" Had it not been for the familiar smell of roses and leather—the scent of pride—Sadie might have forgotten she was there.

"Uh-huh."

Lindsey pinched one of the yellow flowers on her Cat's Claw choker and lowered her gaze. Sadie reached for her own. Their matching necklaces marked their friendship and feline pride. Two things Sadie's parents seemed to know nothing about.

"What did you call it again?" Sadie pressed. "It was so funny. Do you remember?"

Lindsey shrugged.

"You said you were giving me a mane-over. Then, when it was done, you said, 'What a mane-changer.'"

"That was Taylor," she muttered, her green eyes glistening with tears.

"Was it? Oh, well, you're always so funny, so I assumed it was you."

Was Sadie laying it on too thick? Yes. Yes, she was. But only because Lindsey was laying it on thin, and Sadie wanted to prove that her best friend wasn't a total downer.

She placed her hand on Lindsey's shoulder. "Tell my parents what you said last night about the sound of frogs."

Lori's eyes went straight to Lindsey's shoulder, then to Sadie's hand. "What's with those nails?"

"Lindsey is, like, next level at manicures. She got me to stop biting my claws."

"Claws?"

"Maybe you should start again," Dean muttered. "Are those black stripes down the middle *supposed* to be there?"

"They are," Sadie said, struggling to hold her smile.

She could have explained that "those black stripes" meant she was part of the Pack—the most powerful friend group at Charm House. That only four girls were in it, and Sadie was one of them. But her parents were so critical, the opposite of how she described them. It was hard to find words.

"So, Lindsey," Lori began, "what do your parents think about"—she waved a hand at Lindsey's tiger-striped hair—"that?"

"Mom!"

Lindsey rolled back her shoulders and lifted her chin. "My parents don't care what I look like," she said. "I guess I'm lucky that way." Then she excused herself to go to the bathroom.

Once Lindsey was out of earshot, Sadie hissed, "Seriously? Why did you mention her parents?"

This time Lori looked like the anguished emoji. "Was I not supposed to?"

"No!" Sadie snapped, even though it wasn't entirely Lori's fault. She had told her mother that Lindsey's parents were late because they missed their flight; Lindsey, too proud for pity, insisted on it.

If only Sadie could tell them the truth: that Lindsey believed she'd been abandoned. That she felt alone and unloved. Lori might have offered her a free energy healing session, a heart-opening mantra, or a lavender-scented hug. She might have been nice.

"Let's just head over to the barn," Sadie managed. "The showcase is going to start, and I told Taylor and Amy we'd save them seats."

"Are Taylor and Amy your friends?" Dean asked.

Sadie nodded.

He pulled her close. "I look forward to meeting them."

"Yeah, I bet you do," Sadie muttered.

Sadie hadn't entered the barn since her Charm Ceremony six weeks earlier. Since then, the magic carousel that identified her lion-light had been replaced by rows of chairs and a velvet-curtained stage. Still, memories of her black-cloaked class-mates chanting as that carousel spun came rushing back. Though terrifying at first, the ceremony became the best thing that ever happened to Sadie. It got her a pack of best friends, a boyfriend, and a mane-over. Being named top of the food chain could do that to a girl. But the two anguish emojis sitting next to her didn't see it that way.

Sadie waved Taylor's and Amy's families over as Miss Flora took the stage.

"Welcome to the Charm House Family Day showcase," the headmistress began. She paused while everyone hissed their approval. Most parents knew not to clap, as applause was painfully loud to the lights with sensitive ears. Their daughters quickly elbowed those who messed up.

"As always," she continued, "our mission is to teach these powerful young women how to lead happy and productive lives in the real world. Learning how to tame their animal instincts, and work well with others, is crucial." The strict edges of Miss Flora's silver bob swung alongside her jaw as she spoke. "This is why Norma Shepard, our wonderful Typical Topics profes-sor, created Charm Clubs. Not only can our girls explore their passions, but they can also practice teamwork, leadership, and collaboration. We are so very proud of them, and you will be, too, once you see the incredible things they're doing."

Amy, Taylor, and Sadie leaned past their parents and exchanged satisfied smiles. When it came to the Claw Spa, "incredible" was an understatement.

"Are you in a club?" Sadie's father whispered. A contractor, he wore flannel shirts that carried the permanent scent of sawdust.

"Claw Spa," she whispered back. "We offer beauty services."

"Hmm."

"What?" Sadie asked, even though she knew. Dean's *Hmm*s meant he was disappointed.

"Why not a reading club?"

"Yeah," Lori whispered, "you used to love reading."

Sadie couldn't remember the last time she'd opened a book, for school or otherwise. "I still do. It's just that—"

"Our first presentation is from the fashion club," Miss Flora announced.

Sadie sat up a little taller, hoping to redirect her parents' attention away from her and onto the stage.

"These two innovators have redesigned our school uniform because they're, and I quote, 'tired of dressing like safari guides.'" Miss Flora tittered awkwardly as the students hissed with delight. Not only were their existing sand-beige jumpsuits ill-fitting and unflattering, but they were also annoying. A girl shouldn't have to undo seven buttons, wiggle her arms out of the sleeves, then keep said sleeves from falling in the toilet every time she had to pee. That's not a uniform; it's a punishment.

"Please give a big Charm House hiss for Giraffic Park!"

Taylor leaned past her parents, both of whom were checking their emails, and asked, "What does a park have to do with redesigning school uniforms?"

Before Sadie could respond, the lights dimmed and "Girl Like Me" by the Black Eyed Peas and Shakira began to play.

The velvet curtains yawned open, and Gia and Jasmine, both giraffe-lights, strutted out to the song's clap-happy beat, looking nothing like safari guides. What had once been ankle-skimming pants had been cut into a micro miniskirt (Gia) and short-shorts (Jasmine) to show off their endless legs. The sleeves were capped, the shoulders padded, and their names had been written across their backs in colorful sequins. And those seven buttons? Gia's had been removed and replaced with a zipper; Jasmine's had just been removed.

Lori gasped. "How is this appropriate?"

"Chill out, Mom. She's wearing a bikini top," Sadie snipped. Not because she wanted to defend Jasmine—she thought the style was inappropriate, too—but because she was starting to take her parents' disapproval personally. If they didn't understand her friends, they didn't understand *her*.

Amy, however, was all smiles and fangs. She was dancing in her seat, blow-dried hair bouncing with joy as she and her parents exchanged adoring glances that seemed to say:

I love you.

No, I love YOU.

Well, I love you more.

Well, I love you MOST.

Taylor had a certain glow about her, too; only hers was from the glare of her parents' cell phones. At least Lori and Dean cared enough to criticize.

When Miss Flora introduced the Flash Lights, Taylor's expression took on a different kind of glow. This one was lit by something deep inside her.

"Are you ready to tummmm-ble?" shouted Aubrey, a bony lizard-light who had accused Amy of turning her back on her fellow reptiles to become a cat-kisser. And yet, there she was, leading a dance troupe made of monkey-lights. If Amy was bothered by Aubrey's hypocrisy, she didn't show it. She was too busy thumb-wrestling with her younger brother.

"I said," Aubrey shouted again, "are you ready to tummm-ble?"

Techno music began pulsing from the speakers, and five girls dressed in matching leotards bounded onto the stage. What followed was a fast-paced routine full of synchronized fist pumps, pivots, and flips. Captivating as it was, Sadie's attention was on Taylor, who was tracking the performers' moves without a single blink, her tapping feet mirroring their every step. Taylor wasn't just watching the Flash Lights; she was practically dancing with them.

Aubrey sashayed toward center stage for her solo, and

Taylor leaned even closer. Something big was about to happen. A series of aerials, perhaps? A pop? A lock? A tutt? A Waack?

Unfortunately, Sadie never found out. Before Aubrey hit her mark, she rolled her left ankle and fell to the ground. Face tight with pain, she curled into the fetal position and began to rock. The music stopped, Nurse Walker rushed the stage, and the curtains closed. Taylor leaned back in her chair, the bluish-white glow of her parents' phones returning to her face.

Cackle, the hyena-lights' comedy club, were the next and final act in the showcase.

"Hey, Mia," Liv began. "What do you call a kitten that works for the Red Cross?"

"I don't know, Liv. What?"

"A first-aid kit!"

After five minutes of corny animal jokes, the audience got restless. Then Val took over. "A word of advice," she said. "If you're ever at the beach without an umbrella, find a lion, a tiger, a chameleon, or a snake and sit with them."

"Why?" Liv and Mia asked.

"Because they're shady!"

Huh?

"Speaking of *Sadie*," Liv said. "Why did the matador wave his red cape at a lion?"

Val and Mia shrugged.

"Because she was charging!"

Sadie's heart began to race. This was getting personal.

"Charging?" Mia said. "I thought lions pounced."

"Only when you refuse to do their chores."

Sadie, Taylor, and Amy exchanged a nervous glance.

"I'm confused," Mia said. "Why would a lion expect anyone to do her chores?"

"It's the new claw," Val said.

"Claw?" Liv asked.

"Sorry, did I saw claw? I meant law. The one that says you can't get a service at Claw Spa unless you do the Pack's chores and give them your desserts."

"Actually?" Mia said, trying her best to act surprised. "That can't be true."

"It is. I'm not *lion*."

All three of them took a step forward, linked arms, then bowed.

The audience offered up a polite hiss, though they were more confused than amused.

Miss Flora included. She returned to the podium, grinning the way one does when they're enduring a gas pain. "What a wonderful display of talent," she managed. "Thank you, everyone, for—"

"Is that true?" a man shouted. "I pay to send my daughter to this school so she can be safe. Not so she can clean up after other students!"

"I assure you," Miss Flora said, "that is not the case."

"Sure sounds like it is!" a woman called.

"This is unethical!"

"It's obscene."

"It's criminal!"

"It's exploitation!"

"It's inhumane."

Twenty minutes later, Sadie was in Miss Flora's office with her glaring parents, Professor Normal, and one very bothered headmistress.

"I have never been so humiliated," Miss Flora said. There was a slight growl in her voice that only Sadie could detect. Did anyone else know the headmistress was lion-light, or was that a secret between her and Sadie? Either way, Sadie wasn't about to let that cat out of the bag. She was already in enough trouble. "You're a leader," she continued. "And with that comes responsibility and an obligation to follow the rules."

Sadie wanted to explain that Claw Spa, unlike the other clubs, offered a service that most girls were happy to pay for. That they were following the basic principles of supply-and-demand economics, and expecting her to work without compensation was un-American.

"She told me her services were free," Professor Normal said as she paced alongside Miss Flora's desk. Then she sighed. "I knew this was a bad idea."

"You knew *what* was a bad idea?" Dean asked.

"I shouldn't have allowed Sadie to run this club or even participate in it. Her grades are already suffering and—"

"Suffering?" Lori turned to her daughter. Her orange-brown eyes were narrowing. "You said you were doing well."

"I am," Sadie told her. "I've never been better."

"Hmm," Dean said.

"What does that mean?" Lori snipped.

"What does *what* mean?"

"That passive-aggressive *hmm* sound you make. If you want to say something to your daughter, Dean, please come out and say it."

Dean folded his arms across his chest. "What exactly is it that you think I'm not saying, Lori? Not that it matters. You'll end up speaking for me, anyway. Just like you always do."

Sadie sank a little deeper in her chair. Did they have to fight *now*? In front of her teachers?

"I speak for you because you don't have the courage to speak for yourself."

"Stop fighting!" Sadie shouted. She wanted to roar. Run. Throw something. But Miss Flora cut her a look. *Control your instincts.*

Sadie closed her eyes and practiced the deep-breathing technique from Professor Jo's class. When they fluttered open, she glimpsed a trace of approval on Miss Flora's face. She was learning. The headmistress was proud.

"What your father is *trying* to say," Lori said, "is that you've changed. Your grades, your hair, your interests, your priorities . . ." She took a deep breath. "Maybe Charm House isn't the best fit for you."

Sadie jumped to her feet. "Charm House is the only fit for me. I love it here."

"Sometimes loving something doesn't mean it's right," Lori said, eyes on Dean, voice sharp with regret.

"What other options does she have?" Dean asked. "She was expelled from public school."

"Mr. Samson is right," Miss Flora said. "Sadie's instincts are still too wild. And, well, we know what happens to girls who can't control their animal instincts."

Miss Flora didn't have to say it. They all knew. Institute of Behavioral Science is what happened.

"I can homeschool her," Lori tried.

"What? Mom, no. What about your yoga studio? You can't give that up."

Lori reached for her daughter's hand and pulled her close. "For you? Of course I could."

Sadie's eyes filled with tears. She could hear her heart pounding and Miss Flora's, too.

"What about a probation period?" Miss Flora offered. "A chance to improve her grades *and* her attitude?"

"Yes!" Sadie said, unaware of what, exactly, that would entail. Not that it mattered. Sadie would do anything to stay.

"You realize you'll have to find another club, because the Claw Spa is over," Professor Normal added. "And if you fail . . ."

"I won't fail. I promise!"

"Not failing is not good enough," Lori said. "You have to get your grade-point average up to a B-plus by the end of the semester, or we're pulling you from Charm House."

"I will."

"And wash your hair."

"I will."

"And cut your nails."

"I will."

"And start reading."

"I will."

"And be the leader of a club that doesn't exploit anyone."

"I will!"

With a defeated sigh, Lori and Dean agreed to give Sadie one more chance.

"So much for landing on your feet," Professor Normal whispered as they left Miss Flora's office.

It was meant to be a dig, but Sadie refused to let it bring her down. This cat had nine lives, and hers were just getting started.

four

Sadie never chose to go to the Den before; the Den always chose her.

It was in a secret room behind the Watering Hole (a eucalyptus-scented spa filled with soaking tubs) and built just for her. At least that's what the Whisper told her. And yes, the Whisper was literally a whisper.

From what Sadie understood, the wise, all-knowing voice lived inside the cave to teach Sadie how to become a leader. It usually summoned her with the sound of burbling water—a sound that grew louder and more burbly until Sadie dropped what she was doing and paid it a visit. It was kind of like her grandmother that way. But tonight was different. Tonight, it was Sadie who made the first move.

While everyone slept off the excitement of Family Day, Sadie crept toward the rainbow-colored pond at the base of the cave and dipped her toe. As always, the liquid transformed into sand, and the bottom of the rock slid open. Inside, a fire whooshed to life.

"Welcome to the Den, Lion," whispered the female voice. "Trouble sleeping, huh?" She said it like she knew. The Whisper was gifted that way, gifted and a bit creepy.

"The whole nocturnal thing is still a struggle, but this isn't that." She settled onto the heap of pillows by the fire and released a gusty exhale. The flames fluttered. "I need some advice."

"About your grades?"

"No."

"The new club?"

"No."

"Your parents?"

"No," Sadie said. "Revenge."

The flames fluttered again; it was Whisper who sighed this time.

"How is revenge a productive use of your time?"

"The hyenas ratted us out, shut down our spa, and almost got me kicked out of school. It's a productive use of my time because I can't focus on anything else until I pay them back."

"And you want my advice?"

Sadie sat up a little taller. "I do."

"Focus on your grades."

Sadie snickered. "That's it?"

"That's it."

The Whisper's calm, wannabe-soothing tone was irritating. She was supposed to help Sadie channel her inner lion, teach her how to fight back, show her how to intimidate her enemies and rule the school. She was supposed to be on Sadie's side! The hyenas blew up Sadie's world with their nasty little comedy routine. And the Whisper expected Sadie to focus on *grades*? What kind of advice was that?

"Claw Spa got shut down because of them!"

"No, Sadie, Claw Spa got shut down because of you. *You* broke the rules."

"Yeah, but no one knew about it until their stupid comedy show."

"They didn't handle it well, I agree. But Claw Spa's successes—and failures—are its leader's responsibility. So the real question is: What have you learned from this?"

Learned?

I've learned that Val, Liv, and Mia are the real mistake, and I'm going to correct it, whether you like it or not. Sadie didn't say any of that. But she thought it.

"Why don't you let Miss Flora deal with Cackle," the Whisper suggested, as if reading Sadie's mind. "You focus on joining a new club."

Sadie bristled. "I'm supposed to be a leader, not a joiner."

Yes, that sounded obnoxious. But whose fault was that? The Charm House professors had been teaching Sadie how to be a leader for the last six weeks. *Not* saying it would have been worse.

"I like your attitude." The Whisper sounded pleased.

"How about starting your own club. A new club. Show everyone what a strong, *honest* leader you can be."

Sadie was grateful for a second chance, but what kind of club could she possibly lead? Reading was her favorite hobby. But a book club? Really? As a lion-light, she was expected to exude a different kind of energy. Something fierce and aggressive. Something physical. "What kind of club?"

"Something that speaks to your strengths."

Strengths? What did that mean, exactly? Sadie had exceptional hearing, strength, eyesight, and could stay up all night. An exclusive club for lions would have made the most sense. She could name it the Cub Club or the Night Club or the Bacon Club. They could play hunting games, work on tree-climbing skills, sharpen their senses, and eat bacon. But Sadie and Miss Flora were the only lion-lights at Charm House. So now what?

She wanted to run back to her room and forget all about her midnight trip to the Den—run so quickly that she altered the space-time continuum, turned back the clock, and made herself stay in bed. Instead, an electrifying *zing* shot up her spine.

"What about a running club?"

"Hmm," the Whisper said.

Sadie immediately thought of her father and his annoying *hmms*. "What?"

"Do you enjoy running?"

"I'm good at it."

"Yes, but do you *enjoy* it? Does it speak to you?"

"*Speak* to me?"

"Will a running club inspire your inner lion to mature and grow?"

"Sure," Sadie lied. She would have agreed to a toilet-scrubbing club if it meant she could stay at Charm House. "I'll let Miss Flora know in the morning. Thanks, bye!"

With that, Sadie hurried out of the Den and dashed back to her dorm room, leaving the Whisper no time to call her bluff.

Miss Flora lifted her coffee mug to her mouth, then paused. "A running club?"

"Yes." Sadie helped herself to a seat on the couch. Normally she would have opted for one of the high-back chairs facing Miss Flora's desk, but that's where she was sitting yesterday when her mother threatened to take her home. It was bad luck.

"Have any of your peers expressed interest in a running club?" She said "running club" how most people would say "ball of snot"—something to be avoided.

"I haven't asked. I thought I'd talk to you first," Sadie said in her most cooperative tone. "I'm sure Lindsey, Amy, and Taylor will be into it. I mean, it's not like they're busy with Claw Spa anymore, right?" She laughed a little, hoping to put the club conversation behind them and focus on revenge.

"Speaking of Lindsey." Miss Flora lowered the mug onto her desk with a humorless *thunk*. "She didn't show up this morning to take her elixir. That's the second time she's missed a dose this week. If she misses another one, she's going to remember . . ." She circled her desk, sat on the edge, and crossed her stockinged legs. Then she leaned closer to Sadie and, in a calm voice, said, "If she recognizes her mother and me, it will be devastating."

"I know, but—" Sadie stopped herself. This was none of her business. At the same time, Miss Flora *made* it her business.

"But *what*?"

"No offense, Miss Flora, but lying to Lindsey is already devastating."

The headmistress removed her red-framed glasses. Her dark eyes appeared smaller without them, the skin around them more wrinkled. "I'm not following."

"Lindsey was so sad yesterday. Maybe if she knew the truth—"

Miss Flora drew back her head and roared, "NO!" like only a lion-light could.

Sadie gripped the couch cushions so hard her knuckles turned white. Had there been any pictures on the stone walls, they would have crashed to the floor.

"Sorry," Miss Flora muttered. She put on her glasses, smoothed her skirt, and stood. "Truth is not an option, Sadie. Not yet. Not until Lindsey can control her instincts."

Said the woman who just roared, Sadie wanted to say. Instead, she vowed to keep the secret, promised to make Lindsey show up for her appointments, then got back to the real issue. "So, about Cackle—"

"I'll deal with them." Miss Flora returned to her desk, jiggled her computer mouse, and fixed her attention on the screen.

"How, exactly?" Sadie pressed. Was she out of line? Yes! No one bossed the boss. But Miss Flora was desperate for Sadie's help with Lindsey, and so long as she was, Sadie felt safe making demands. If only her pack mates had been there to see it. They would have been so impressed.

"Good luck with your running club," Miss Flora said, fingers clacking on her keyboard. "I look forward to seeing what you do with that."

"Thanks. Oh, and in case you need some punishment ideas, I have a few thoughts—"

"I said I'll deal with them," Miss Flora growled.

"But—"

"Being tardy for breakfast is no way to get your grades up, Miss Samson."

And being on time is?

Miss Flora removed those red glasses of hers, glared at Sadie, and through gritted teeth said, "Go!"

And that was the end of that.

For now.

five

"**Y**ou want us to join a *what*?" Amy asked as she sank her fangs into a snickerdoodle cookie.

"A running club," Sadie announced. She had spread her comforter on the back lawn and laid out a buffet of sugary snacks, hoping the rush of glucose would motivate them to lace up and follow her lead.

"Mmmm." Amy chewed. "For a minute, I thought you said a 'rund ink lub,' which would have made more sense."

It was a sunny Monday afternoon. Class had just let out, and the girls were given thirty minutes of freedom before they had to report to their Charm Club leaders. Sadie had exactly twenty-seven minutes to sell her idea to the Pack.

"Why would we want to run?" Lindsey asked. She was lying on her back, gazing up at the cloud-streaked sky.

"Why wouldn't you? It's a heart-healthy activity, a great way to release stress, and thanks to Cackle, we need a new club. Plus we are the fastest lights in school. It will be easy."

"Running is for scared people," Lindsey quipped.

"I don't hear any other ideas."

Two heartbeats began to quicken. Sadie held her breath and used her powerful lion hearing to figure out who among them was afraid. It was Amy and Taylor. "Um, anything you guys want to tell me?"

Amy glanced back at the school. Taylor leaned forward and touched her toes. Maybe she did want to run. Only she didn't say that. She didn't say anything. Neither of them did.

"They already joined clubs," Lindsey blurted.

Sadie jerked back her head. "No, they didn't."

"Yes, they did."

"Didn't."

"Did."

"Not."

"Yot."

Yot?

"They seriously joined other clubs?"

"Um, hello," Taylor said, straightening. "We're right here."

Sadie narrowed her eyes and looked at her friends, really looked at them. These friends she called family; how could they move on so quickly and not even tell her? Their expressions gave nothing away, and yet something about their appearances seemed different. Something right below the surfaces of their skin. A current of energy, a glow. As if electricity had been restored after a power outage.

"Which clubs did you join?" Sadie managed.

"You know how Aubrey rolled her ankle during the show-case?" Taylor began.

Sadie nodded. Or maybe she didn't. Her thoughts were tangled, her senses dulled.

"Well, she's on crutches, and the Flash Lights need a choreographer."

"So they asked you?"

Taylor folded forward again. "Sort of."

"She asked *them*," Lindsey offered with a pot-stirring smile.

Sadie's muscles tensed. Typical chameleon. Always changing herself to fit in. "Why didn't you tell me?"

"IlovedancingandClawSpawasdoneandIhadnoideayou'd bestartinganewcluband—"

"It's okay." Sadie sighed because she *wanted* it to be okay. But it didn't *feel* okay. It felt like betrayal and smelled bitter, like tarnished silver.

She turned her attention on Amy. "What club did you join?"

"I didn't join one; I started one." She offered a nervous smile, lips covering her fangs.

The tarnished silver smell intensified. Sadie clutched her stomach. "What is it?" *And why didn't you ask me to join?*

"It's a tutoring club. I help people who are having a hard time in school."

"I know what tutoring is," Sadie snapped.

"Sorry." Amy's pale skin flushed. "I have my first appointment in five minutes, so I better get going." She helped herself to another snickerdoodle and stuffed it in her yellow fanny pack.

Taylor stood. "Same."

Before leaving, Amy looked over her shoulder and smiled. "I can help you with your grades if you want. Just let me know when. I'm booking up quickly. But you get priority. Obviously."

"I'm good," Sadie muttered. "I need to focus on my club, so . . ." She gave a playful whack to Lindsey's muscular leg. "Looks like it's just us. You in?"

"You joking?"

Sadie removed her hand. "Why would I be joking?"

"Because it doesn't matter what I do."

"Of course it—"

"No, Sadie, it doesn't. Unlike you, I don't have parents who care about my grades. I'm going to kick back for a while and coast."

Sadie felt that familiar dip in her belly. The one that always showed up when she was ignoring the truth. "Did you take your elixir today?"

Lindsey stood and hooked her backpack over her shoulder. "What does that have to do with anything?"

"It's supposed to help you remember your parents."

"Yeah, well, it doesn't." She began walking toward the woods. "Good luck with your running club."

"Wait, where are you going?"

"To see Link. He has football practice at three-thirty."

Sadie felt another dip in her stomach. This one was born out of fear. "Miss Flora said we couldn't go to practices. Only supervised games. You'll get in major trouble if she finds out. Or worse." She didn't have to explain what "worse" meant. Lindsey knew that IBS hunted animal-lights, that they captured Kate in these very woods. Lindsey lived with that threat every day. They all did. She *knew*.

"If anyone asks, say I'm in your running club," Lindsey said. Then she sped off on her tiger-strong legs and was out of sight in seconds.

Limbs heavy with disappointment, Sadie began sealing up the uneaten cookies and folding her comforter. The meeting was over, just like her future. So much for the *Paws, Claws, and Jaws* pact they'd made a few weeks earlier, where they painted matching black stripes on their fingernails and pledged their loyalty. Ha! Sadie didn't feel secure. She felt alone.

Alone and desperate.

The running club needed at least two members to qualify, and everyone was spoken for. Everyone except Sondra and Kara, who told Professor Normal that no one had room for them. When really they were too lazy to commit to anything. But what if they had no choice?

"What do you mean I *owe* you?" Sondra asked Sadie ten minutes later. They were standing in the open doorway of Sondra's dorm room. Behind her, Kara was lying on her bed, pretending to nap, dingo ears wiggling as she eavesdropped.

"You were supposed to do our laundry this morning." Sadie cut a look to Sondra's ombré hair. "You promised."

"Miss Flora said all chores owed to Claw Spa employees were null and void."

"True, but you're still indebted to us. You both are," Sadie said loud enough for Kara to hear. "But don't worry. I have an idea."

As they stood at the edge of the forest, stretching for their inaugural run, Sadie told herself not to obsess over her club members' wardrobe choices. But really, Sondra? A miniskirt? And, Kara, on what planet do lace-up riding boots make sense? Not that Sadie said a word. At least they showed up.

"So what exactly is the objective of this club?" Kara asked.

To keep me from getting homeschooled by my mother. To check on Lindsey and make sure she's okay. To try and forget that the Pack moved on without me. "To make new friends and bond while exercising outdoors," Sadie finally said.

"And we're supposed to do all that while we *run*?" Sondra said. "With *you*?"

"What's wrong with me?"

Sondra indicated her skinny legs, then Kara's short ones. "We're not built like you."

"We're going to take this slow and easy," Sadie assured them. "This isn't a competition. It's about bonding in nature."

Sondra and Kara nodded, and Sadie felt hopeful for the first time all day.

"Where are we going, boss?" Kara asked as she tightened her laces.

Sadie's spirit soared—at least *someone* respected her. "The Allendale football field."

"All the way to Allendale?" Sondra whined. "That's, like, three miles. Maybe more."

"We'll take it easy," Sadie said with a can-do wave. "Come on. It'll be fun."

Sadie arrived at the football field nine minutes later. She didn't mean to take off and had every intention of sticking together. But her legs had a mind of their own, and those leg-minds needed to move.

Panting, she scanned the woods for Sondra and Kara, but they were still too far away to track. Instead, she turned her attention to the field, where dozens of boys grunted their way through warm-up drills. Lindsey was nowhere to be found.

Not on the bleachers. Not leaning against the goalpost. Not working out with the boys, flirting. *Nowhere.*

Sadie considered the worst-case scenario. *What will I do if IBS has Lindsey? Who can I tell? How will I forgive myself for watching her go?*

Then Sadie spotted Beak, and a different kind of terror took hold.

What was he doing on the field? And why was her bookworm boyfriend wearing a football uniform?

six

"*Y*ou joining the football team is not a surprise. It's a bomb drop," Sadie told Beak.

He was on a five-minute water break and had run over to say hi. His cheeks were flushed, and his usual grape-eraser scent was seasoned with something salty, a brininess that Sadie would start associating with the smell of being duped.

Beak was a reader, not a jock. He was going to sit on the bleachers with Sadie and share popcorn while fans cheered for whatever fans cheer for in football. He was supposed to choose Sadie, not the sport; give her the attention her father never did. Now what was she going to do during the Allendale games? Watch?

"Speaking of bomb-drop," he said, voice cracking with puberty. "You changed your hair."

Sadie looked down at the muddy tips of his cleats. She knew Beak would notice her ombré color but never suspected he'd find it shocking. Not that his opinion should matter.

(But it did.)

Beak made Sadie feel feelings she didn't know she had. Tingly feelings. Bubbly feelings. Feelings that conjured the dancing mist on a freshly poured soda. Every text he wrote, every selfie he sent, every smile he flashed tickled her belly in ways that bacon never could. And she didn't want one bit of that to end.

"When did you change it?" he asked in that way that sounded more like *why*.

"A few days ago. It's not permanent or anything."

He took a massive gulp of water and licked his berry-red lips. "Cool."

"Cool that it's not permanent?"

"No." Beak grinned. "It looks cool."

Mist danced. "Actually?"

"Yeah." Beak had the same emerald-green eyes as Lindsey, only hers were fierce and his were friendly. "It makes me think of those half-chocolate, half-vanilla cookies."

"Is that a good thing?" Sadie dared.

"It is." He grinned again. "I love those cookies."

A rush of heat shot up the back of Sadie's neck. Her armpits prickled. If Beak thought of those cookies when he looked at her hair and loved those cookies, did that mean he loved *her*? And if so, was Sadie supposed to say *I love those cookies too*? Because she did.

But speaking was not an option. Beak's smile was too adoring, his gaze too fixed. If they were in a Netflix original teen movie, he would have leaned forward and kissed her. But

Sadie wasn't sure if she was ready for that. Yet, at the same time, she wasn't sure she *wasn't.*

"When did you start playing football?" she managed.

"I used to play with my dad . . ." he began; then his voice trailed off. Probably because his dad, aka Karl Van der Beak, aka the medical director of IBS, didn't know Lindsey, his daughter, was a tiger-light and would probably experiment on her if he did. No wonder Beak didn't want to talk about him.

"Cool uniform," Sadie said, changing the subject.

"Really? You seemed a little freaked by it."

"I wasn't expecting it, that's all. I'm . . ." Sadie stopped herself. What she wanted to say was *I'm used to seeing you in slouchy pants and sloppy sweaters, but you should wear clothes that fit better because they show off your muscles, and you have outstanding muscles.* Sadie wouldn't say any of those things, ever. "It's cute" was the best she could do.

"Cute?" Beak snickered. "Just what every football player wants to hear."

Sadie laughed a little too hard for a little too long. So much was being said by the things they weren't saying. She didn't dare add more words.

"So where are your pom-poms?" he asked. His face was flushed, but the C-shaped scar on his cheek remained white.

"Huh?"

"Aren't you here to cheer for me?" Beak said with that teasing half-smile of his.

"It's a practice."

"Still, a little support would be nice."

"Don't you have cheerleaders for that?"

"We had tryouts last week, but none of the boys were good enough," he joked.

Peeeeep!

The coach blew his whistle.

"Break is over," Beak sighed. He lifted the bottom of his jersey and wiped the sweat from his forehead. Lucky uniform.

"Where's your ring?" Sadie asked, mainly because the gold band on his thumb was missing, but also because she wasn't ready to say goodbye.

"Coach said I couldn't wear it while I played." He reached into his back pocket, then poked his hand through the chain-link fence that separated them. "Want to hold on to it for me?"

Sadie shrugged as if too cool to care either way. "Sure." She slid it onto her thumb but felt its weight behind her belly.

"Wait," he said, suddenly serious. "I never asked why you're really here."

She was about to share the tragic truth about her running club but was interrupted by the sound of a girl's laughter.

It was Lindsey, hurrying up the fence, while Link, her crush, squirted her with his water bottle.

Those friendly green eyes of Beak's turned fierce. "What is *she* doing here?"

"I tried to stop her, but—"

"But what?" he snapped. "She can't be out here. She draws too much attention to herself. Sadie, you're supposed to protect her."

The dancing mist dissolved. That weight behind her belly turned to nausea. Did he have to say her name like that?

Peeeeep. Peeeeep.

The coach's whistle blew before Sadie had a chance to defend herself. Not that she could have. *It's not fair that your family made Lindsey my responsibility* probably wouldn't fly.

"Link, Van der Beak! Let's go!"

"Get her out of here," Beak told Sadie. "Hurry."

They parted ways without saying goodbye, which felt like getting fries without ketchup. Their exchange was filling but it lacked zing.

"We gotta go," Sadie said the moment Lindsey jumped over the fence. She took her by the wrist and yanked her back into the woods.

"Stop," Lindsey insisted, trying to wiggle free. "I don't want to—"

Sadie tightened her grip. "The coach saw us, and if he tells Miss Flora—"

"I don't care."

When they got to the clearing, Sadie stopped to catch her breath. "You have to care," she panted. "What if you get caught?"

Lindsey lifted her face to the cloudless sky and grinned. "Totally worth it."

"Climbing a fence to see Link was worth risking our football game privileges? Worth risking our lives?"

"No." Lindsey grinned. "Getting my first kiss was."

Sadie gasped, then whacked Lindsey on the arm. "Pause!"

Lindsey held out her hand and splayed her fingers.

"Not those paws," Sadie giggled. "I meant pause as in tell me everything. What was it like? Were you nervous? Did you know what to do?" She closed her fist around Beak's thumb ring and squeezed. "How did it even happen?"

"It wasn't a big deal," she said, trying to sound chill. "I hopped the fence and told Link I've always wanted to kiss a football player."

Sadie whacked her on the arm again. "You said that?"

"Yeah, why?"

"What if he said no?"

Lindsey held Sadie by the shoulders and looked deep into her eyes. "That would never happen."

Sadie giggled. "Good point."

Back at Charm House, Sondra and Kara were sunning themselves on the back lawn.

"There you are," Sondra said as the girls emerged from the woods.

"What are you doing lying around?" Sadie asked, remembering that she had forgotten all about them.

"Quitting," Kara answered, still supine.

"Why?"

"You abandoned us."

Lindsey scoffed. "This is your running club?"

Sadie nodded, ashamed.

"You can't quit," Lindsey told them.

"Why not?" Sondra asked.

"Because you're fired!"

"You can't fire us!" Sondra said. "You're not even in the club."

Kara scratched the backs of her ears. "Anyway, what did *we* do?"

"You run like sloth-lights and—"

Sadie quickly pulled Lindsey aside. "What are you doing? I need them."

"No, you don't. You need to sneak out with me and kiss Beak. This whole club thing is—"

"Stop," Sadie growled. "We can't sneak out."

Lindsey put her hands on her hips. "How else are we going to hang with them? Start a football team?"

Sadie cocked her head. They were certainly fast enough and at least ten times stronger. But a pack of middle school girls crushing a boy's football team was a news headline in the making. And attention was the last thing they needed. But what if . . .

"I have two words for you."

"Quarterback?" Lindsey said.

"That's one word."

"Team captain?"

"No."

"Ditch school?"

"No! Cheerleading club."

Lindsey rolled her eyes. "Ew. Enough with your clubs."

"Think about it," Sadie said. "The Allendale Cougars need cheerleaders. If we started a squad, we could go to all their games and travel with the team. We'd get out of here but in a safe way."

Lindsey pulled Sadie into a suffocating hug. "Puuuuurfect!"

"So you'll join?"

"Twice!" Lindsey beamed.

Sadie laughed. How did that even make sense? "Let's go to Miss Flora's office and sign up. Oh, and you can take your elixir while we're there."

Lindsey was so excited she agreed without hesitation.

"Wait," Kara said as the girls ran off. "What about us?"

"You quit, remember?" Sadie called over her shoulder.

"What if we quit quitting?"

"We don't give a quit!" Lindsey shouted.

Sadie threw her arm around her friend and pulled her close. Beak's ring glinted in the sunlight.

The Pack was back!

seven

Sadie and Lindsey hurried to Miss Flora's office but stopped short of her door.

"Listen," Sadie whispered, leaning in.

Lindsey nodded. She could hear them, too.

They decided to wait across the hall by the water fountain so no one could accuse them of eavesdropping, then perked up their super-sensitive ears and eavesdropped.

"Where's Mia?" (Miss Flora.) *"I want to speak with all of you."*

"She's with her tutor." (Val.)

Lindsey and Sadie exchanged a glance. Was Amy tutoring *Mia?*

"We could come back another time." (Liv.)

"No!" (Miss Flora.) *"But do let her know that yesterday's so-called jokes were far from funny and—"*

"Okay, we will. Thank you. Bye." (Liv.)

"Yeah, have a great rest of your day." (Val.)

"Sit!" (Miss Flora.) *"You girls know better than to razz your*

*fellow lights. And you absolutely know better than to do it in
public. How do you think Sadie, Lindsey, Amy, and Taylor felt?
How do you think their parents felt? How do you think I felt?"*

"We were speaking up against injustice." (Val.) *"Isn't that
what we're supposed to do?"*

*"Once you have your instincts under control, yes. Until then,
come to me. Your material was speciest, and we don't tolerate
that at Charm House."*

Sadie and Lindsey high-fived. Go, Miss Flora, go!

"What about what the Pack did?" (Val.) *"How was that
okay?"*

*"It wasn't. I shut down Claw Spa and will do the same to
Cackle if you don't drop the offensive content. From now on, I
need to approve your act before every show."*

"That's censorship!" (Liv.)

"It's damage control."

*"It's allowing one person to decide what's funny. Shouldn't
we give that power to the audience?"*

Sadie was semi-impressed. Val and Liv weren't going down
without a fight. It was bold and daring, but also kind of dumb.

*"You tried that yesterday. And the audience didn't laugh.
They did, however, lodge several complaints. Some even threatened to remove their kids from Charm House. None of that seems
funny to me. Does it seem funny to you?"*

Sadie and Lindsey covered their mouths to conceal
their giggles.

"Comedy is our way of calling out the injustices of the world. It's no different than journalism."

"It's very different, Liv. Journalism doesn't turn people into punch lines. From now on, Cackle will tell nice jokes or—"

"Nice jokes? Is that even a thing?"

"Of course it is. There are plenty of ways to be funny without targeting people. For example, what kind of instrument is found in the bathroom?"

"A tuba toothpaste," Lindsey said to no one in particular. Then she pressed two fingers against the side of her head and rubbed her temple. "How did I know that?"

Sadie bristled. Miss Flora must have told that joke to Lindsey when she was a little girl. Her memory was coming back; she needed that elixir. "It's a kindergarten classic," Sadie lied. "Everyone knows it."

"We can't tell baby jokes!" (Val.)

"Then you will have to find a new club."

"But—"

"This conversation is over."

"That's censorship."

"No, Val. It's standards."

The office door swung open. Liv and Val walked out in a huff, then slowed when they saw Sadie and Lindsey.

"Look, it's the girls who can't take a joke," Val said as they passed.

"Look, it's the girls who can't make one," Lindsey fired back.

Sadie, determined to stay focused, knocked on Miss Flora's door.

"My word is final!" the headmistress called.

"It's Sadie."

"Not now, dear."

"And Lindsey," Sadie added.

The door yawned open. "Come in."

She was rubbing floral-scented lotion into her hands, perhaps in need of a fresh start. "Are you here to take your elixir?"

"She is," Sadie said before Lindsey could argue.

Miss Flora flashed an appreciative glance at Sadie, then hurried for the shelf behind her desk. It contained several vials of amber liquid marked *L.S. Elixir*.

Sadie's stomach dipped in the bad way. The *L.S.* stood for *Lindsey Striker*. Only, Striker wasn't her real last name; Van der Beak was. It was another lie they were feeding Lindsey in the name of protecting her, another lie Sadie was expected to swallow right along with her.

"Is that jasmine I smell?" Lindsey asked, wincing a little.

"Yes, it's my hand cream," Miss Flora said as she pulled a vial from her shelf. "I've been wearing it since I was your age. It reminds me of simpler times."

Lindsey lowered her head and pressed her fingers into her

temples again. Another flashback. Thankfully, Miss Flora's back was turned and she didn't notice.

"You okay?" Sadie mouthed.

Miss Flora whipped around. She, too, was a lion-light. But, unlike Professor Normal, the headmistress heard it all. "What's wrong with Lindsey?"

"Nothing," Lindsey managed. Then she thanked Miss Flora for the elixir, wrapped her hand around the vial, and drank it down.

"While we're here, there's something we want to talk to you about," Sadie began.

"I've already handled Cackle, as you know." Miss Flora smirked. *You're not the only one with lion-light powers around here,* her expression seemed to say. *I could hear you listening.*

Sadie's cheeks burned with embarrassment. "Actually, it's about our club."

"We want to start a football team," Lindsey blurted.

Sadie shot her a look. Was Lindsey losing her mind? That's not what they discussed.

"A football team?" Miss Flora sat. "And whom, exactly, would you be playing?"

"Allendale."

She leaned forward. "Absolutely not. You'd crush them, and we'd be exposed."

"Hmmm. Good point," Lindsey said with a quick side-eye to Sadie. "I never thought of that." Losing her mind? No.

Lindsey knew precisely what she was doing. "We just wanted to do something physical and outdoors. Something that would allow us to interact *safely* with another school. We behaved at the dance and there hasn't been any drama at the Allendale football games, so we thought—" Lindsey swiped her hand through the jasmine-scented air. "Forget it. It was stupid."

"Wait," Sadie said, playing along. "What about a cheerleading squad?"

Lindsey drew back her head. "A cheerleading squad? Yeah, I don't know."

"Think about it. We'd get the physical-outdoors thing and the interaction thing, but not the risk-of-exposure thing."

"True," Lindsey said.

"Interesting," Miss Flora said with a *tap-tap* on her chin. "Professor Jo and I have been meaning to coordinate more events with Allendale. But I don't know. Do you think you're ready for that?"

"Challenging ourselves is the only way to grow," Sadie said. She stole the line from Professor Jo—a line Professor Jo had probably stolen from Miss Flora. So it had to work. "It will also help us prepare for life in the real world."

"How many girls would be in your squad?"

"Four," Sadie answered. "Just the Pack. We want to keep it small. Small and safe."

"What about the choreography? If you draw on your powers, you will be exposed."

"We won't," Sadie promised. "Typical moves only."

"And traveling to other schools?"

"We'd have a chaperone, Professor Jo, maybe. You know, since she teaches Instinct Control." Sadie raised her eyebrows just enough to remind the headmistress that Professor Jo was also Lindsey's mother and would protect her better than anyone.

Miss Flora removed her red-framed glasses, rubbed her eyes, and sighed. "Lindsey, you would have to take your elixir every day. No more skipping."

"I know."

"And I'd have to check with the football team's coach."

"Of course," Sadie said, as she twirled Beak's ring around her thumb. "Just let us know."

"Nicely played, Sadie Lady," Lindsey said once they were back in the dim hallway. "Looks like your first kiss is right around the corner."

"This isn't about kisses. It's about practicing instinct control," Sadie said in case Miss Flora was listening. But if Miss Flora was half the lioness she claimed to be, she would have heard Sadie's heart speed at the mere thought of kissing Beak. Because yes. A teeny part of her—the lip part—hoped that becoming a cheerleader for the Cougars would give her more time with Beak. Lately, their packed schedules didn't leave any room for hanging out, and she missed him. She missed *them.*

"Wait, this isn't about kisses?" Lindsey said. "Then why are we doing this?"

Sadie stopped walking. "Shhh."

"Don't tell me to—"

"Shhhh!" Sadie insisted. "Smell that?"

Lindsey sniff-sniffed the air. "Wasn't me." Then she stiffened, as if sensing them, too. "Tarnished silver?"

Sadie nodded. Val and Liv were close by. Still bitter, they were probably plotting revenge.

"Whatever," Lindsey said with a dismissive eye roll. "We're four times stronger and can take them down with a single claw swipe. Worst case? We'd need a quick nail touch-up. Totally worth it if you ask me." She leaned over the water fountain as if preparing to drink but didn't push the silver button. Instead, Lindsey pulled the vial of elixir from her pocket and emptied it into the drain.

Sadie gasped. "What are you doing? I thought you drank it already!"

Lindsey lifted a finger to her lips, refusing to respond until they were in the bathroom, all sinks running. "It hasn't helped me remember a single thing about my family. I remember more when I *don't* take it. But try telling that to Miss Flora."

"Have you?"

"Have I what?"

"Have you tried telling that to Miss Flora?"

"A few times," Lindsey said. "But she refuses to believe her special potion doesn't work. So I'll keep letting her think it does. It's easier that way."

With the sink still running, Lindsey flushed the empty vial down the toilet and smiled brightly. "I'm going to figure out who my parents are, Sadie Lady. And when I do, we'll leave this place and live with them. Out there. In the real world. Where no one will try to tame us."

Sadie's eye twitched as she offered Lindsey a supportive thumbs-up. Because now what? Was she supposed to betray her best friend and tell Miss Flora and Beak that Lindsey was fake-taking her elixir? Or betray their trust and keep Lindsey's secret?

If only there were an elixir for Sadie, something to make her forget she'd heard any of that. She'd drink every last drop of it.

Twice.

eight

*I*t was chilly in the chapel, especially in the evenings.
Miss Flora didn't believe in heating rooms that weren't
being used, which was fine for warm-bloods like Sadie and
Lindsey. Even Taylor didn't seem to mind. The cold-blooded
chameleon-light was jogging in place, heating her muscles for
dance club practice. But Amy, also a cold-blood, didn't enjoy
exercise. Power-studying was her workout. So she shivered and
complained instead.

"What's this late-breaking news you're so excited about?"
she asked, fangs chattering. "We were *just* together at dinner.
Why didn't you tell us then?" She zipped her fleece jacket and
stuffed her dry, scaly hands in the pockets.

"What difference does it make?" Sadie was aware of
the slight irritation in her tone. But come on, where was
Amy's sense of adventure? "It's not like you have anything
else to do."

"Wrong. I have a tutoring appointment in twenty minutes."

"Is it Mia?" Sadie asked. Cackle was the reason the Pack

needed a new club in the first place, making Mia one-third of that reason.

"You're tutoring Mia?" Taylor gasped. "A *hyena*? Isn't that a conflict of interest?"

"I can't reveal the identity of my clients. It's confidential."

Lindsey scoffed. "You're a tutor, not a mental health professional."

"Too bad for you," Amy said with a teasing smile.

They arrived at a foreboding wood door in the back of the chapel, and the conversation stopped. Serious and focused, Lindsey lifted the gold nail file around her neck, poked it through the keyhole, and began wiggling it around.

The choir room was the perfect place for Sadie to tell the Pack about her new private cheerleading club. Back when Charm House was a convent, the nuns soundproofed the walls so the choir could rehearse during the priest's sermon without being overheard. As a result, not even the most potent set of animal ears could penetrate the padding.

"Does this have anything to do with whatever Miss Flora whispered to you in the hallway after dinner?" Taylor asked.

Sadie held a silencing finger to her lips and nodded, even though she wanted to shout, *Miss Flora pulled me aside earlier and said the Allendale football coach would stop by on Saturday to see our routine! If he thinks we're good, we can be the official cheerleaders for the Cougars!* Then there were the things Miss Flora told her during that conversation that she wasn't going to say at all. Things like: "It would be nice if you included girls that aren't in your pack. Diversity is crucial when building a team." And, "I trust you will spread the word."

Not that Sadie had a problem including other girls. She didn't. Her problem was leading them. What if Sadie had terrible ideas? What if the Typicals made fun of them and Lindsey attacked? If only they could use their powers—they would be the fiercest squad in the history of fierce squads. But they couldn't.

The way Sadie saw it, fewer people meant fewer problems. Granted, Lindsey, Taylor, and Amy weren't easy to control. Lindsey was a constant flight risk. Taylor was always worrying about something. And Amy had been super secretive lately. But they were her pack. They looked out for one another, and she knew that if something went wrong, they'd laugh.

"Voila!" Lindsey said, removing her nail file from the keyhole.

The door clicked open, and a moldy must rushed out to greet them.

"Ew," Lindsey said, burying her nose in the crook of her elbow. "It smells like an airplane fart in here."

The girls cracked up. They had no idea what Lindsey meant by "airplane fart," which made it even funnier.

Sadie flicked on the lights and shut the door. The windowless room was empty, the gray carpet sad. Forlorn and forgotten, it deserved some good news. They all did. And Sadie was about to give it to them. "Our club problems are over!"

Taylor blink-blinked. "What club problems?"

"We don't have a club," Sadie explained. "And that's a problem."

"Stop saying club," Amy giggled. "It doesn't sound like a word anymore."

"What about *problem*?" Lindsey said. "She keeps saying that, too."

"I know, but that sounds fine."

"Don't you have a running club?" Taylor asked, ignoring Amy's request.

"We're over that," Lindsey said.

"We?" The furrow between Taylor's eyebrows deepened.

"Tell them, Sadie Lady," Lindsey said, beaming with the kind of pride that comes from knowing a secret before it's told. Then she called out, "We're starting a cheerleading club!"

"Lindsey!"

"A cheerleading club?" Amy cocked her head. "For real?"

"Who are you cheering for?" Taylor asked.

"The Allendale Cougars!" Sadie and Lindsey said together.

Amy unzipped her yellow fanny pack and pulled out a vial of her orange and clove-scented oil. "Why would you do *that*?"

"We," Lindsey explained.

"All four of us," Sadie added. "We're going to be their cheerleaders. It's our new club!"

Taylor and Amy exchanged a confused look. Hardly the joyful screams and celebratory backflips Sadie had hoped for.

"And why would we cheer for *them*?" Amy asked, massaging the oil into her hands. "What do *they* do?"

"They play football," Lindsey said.

"So?"

"So now we can go to their games, travel when they play other schools, and kiss football players. We can get out of here!"

Taylor ran her palm over the spiky tips of her pink Mohawk. "I like being here."

"And I don't need to hang out with the Allendale boys every weekend," Amy added. She was only two months younger than Lindsey but light-years behind her when it came to crushes. So during dinner, when Lindsey told them she'd kissed Link, Amy and Taylor were more concerned about Lindsey getting caught than the details.

"It's not about hanging with the Allendale boys," Sadie said. "It's about hanging with us." Her phone began to ring. Beak was FaceTiming. She quickly declined the call.

"Speak for yourself," Lindsey muttered. "Anyway, what else are you going to do?"

"Dance with the Flash Lights," Taylor said while pulling her ankle toward her butt for a quad stretch. "I've been choreographing a mash-up of hip-hop and modern jazz that's just the right amount of hard. Challenging but not impossible, you know?"

Sadie didn't know, but she nodded like someone who did. "Teach those routines to us instead."

Taylor lowered her leg. "You're not dancers."

"True," Lindsey said. "But we need to learn for the squad."

"I'm hypermobile," Amy said. "I could get hurt."

"I'm hyperstrong. I won't let you," Sadie told her. "Come on, this is important. I need the extra credit to get my grades up. If I don't, my parents will make me leave." Those words, when spoken aloud, had a certain thickness to them; they were almost too heavy to get out.

"I could tutor you," Amy offered.

"Or you could join my club."

"But we're already in clubs," Taylor tried.

"Quit," Lindsey told them. It was more of an order than a suggestion.

Taylor's body began to fade and camouflage with the stone wall behind her. "I'm the leader."

"Are you going to scratch your name into their skin if they don't listen to you?" Lindsey blurted.

It was harsh, but Taylor kind of deserved it. They forgave her for attacking them a few weeks earlier, but they didn't forget. And they didn't want her to either.

"I can't just quit," Taylor said, ignoring the dig.

"You can't, or you won't?" Lindsey pressed.

"I like the Flash Lights," she peeped.

"More than you like us?" Sadie's pulse began to race, as if her heart was trying to outrun Taylor's response. It was *that* afraid of getting hurt.

"It's different," she muttered, her body fully invisible. "The Flash Lights listen to me."

"Sadie needs this, you guys," Lindsey pleaded.

They looked at her sideways, knowing that becoming an Allendale cheerleader served Lindsey just as much as Sadie. Sadie and Link. But personal agendas aside, this was going to be fun! Why couldn't Taylor and Amy see that?

"The Allendale coach will be here on Saturday to see our routine. Can we at least try?" Sadie pleaded.

"I can't bail on the Flash Lights," Taylor said. "But what if we let them join our squad?"

"I wish, but Miss Flora wants us to keep it quiet, or else everyone will want to try out. Which would be chaos," Sadie lied. The more lights she was responsible for, the more opportunities she'd have to mess up. "Anyway, this is about the Pack. Yes, the club will help my grade, and yes, Lindsey will be able to leave Charm House every now and then, but this is really about going on adventures together." This was the genuine part. Because when you finally have friends worth making memories with, you want to start making them as soon as possible.

"Are you in or are you out?' Lindsey added, knowing full well that *they* knew full well how challenging life would be if they chose "out."

"Whaddaya say?" Sadie held up her hand and bent her fingers to resemble a paw with claws. It signified solidarity and hearkened their loyalty pact. "Claws, Paws, and Jaws?" she reminded them. Then she began to recite it. "I pledge my soul to the Charm House Pack; I will be honest, true, and have your back . . ."

"The stripes on my nails are my eternal vow," Lindsey said, joining her. "To be fierce, to be loyal, to be the cat's meow. No matter what happens, no matter the cause, I will hold my head high and my paws in claws."

They touched fingertips to seal in the pledge, then turned to Amy and Taylor.

"Can I be the choreographer?" Taylor asked.

"Yes!" Sadie said.

Taylor made a paw with claws.

"Can I be in charge of the practice schedule so I can keep some of my tutoring clients?" Amy asked, shivering.

"Absolutely!"

Amy bent her peace fingers to resemble fangs. "Okay, I'm in."

"That's the spirit!" Sadie bellowed. Then she giggled. "Pun intended."

It wasn't her best joke, or even a good one, but it made them laugh. The whole memory-making thing was off to a great start.

nine

For Sadie, the most stressful part about leading the cheer club was not waking the Pack up before class to practice. It was not hauling four mattresses onto the back lawn in the dark, nor was it trying to sneak out of Charm House undetected. It was convincing the girls to agree on, well, everything else.

"What was the point of bringing our mattresses if you're not even going to *try*?" Taylor asked Amy, white puffs of air spilling from her mouth.

The sky was trying to wake, offering barely there glimpses of the sun. Sun that was shifting the predawn light from black to charcoal but did little in the way of warming things up. Perhaps that's why the cold-bloods were so cranky.

"Why do I have to be the one who gets tossed?" Amy asked. She glanced back at the school as if begging it to rescue her.

"Um, hello, you're fully padded, that's why," Lindsey said, pointing a sharp fingernail at Amy's puffy jacket, two pairs of sweatpants, Uggs, and ski hat.

"Um, hi, I have padding because it's cold out here," Amy said with a slight shiver. "And hypermobile people should not be cold while exercising. It can lead to injuries." She looked to Sadie this time, gray eyes wide and pleading. *A little help, please!*

"You're getting tossed because you're the lightest one here," Sadie calmly explained (for what felt like the tenth time).

"Um, hello, nice try. You and Lindsey are strong enough to toss the Rock."

"Yeah, but no one can know that," Sadie said. "We need to look Typical, remember?"

According to her research, there were three prominent cheerleading positions: flyers, basers, and spotters. The flyers get thrown by the basers and are kept safe by the spotters. Since Sadie and Lindsey were the strongest, they were the basers. Taylor, the spotter, was responsible for ensuring that they were positioned correctly so the flyer could stick the landing. In theory, it made perfect sense. But in practice, not so much.

"Taylor's only, like, five pounds heavier than I am," Amy argued. "Why can't we toss *her*?"

"Three pounds," Taylor corrected. "And it's all height."

"When?" Amy asked.

"When, what?"

Amy giggled. "When did I ask you?"

They shared a quick laugh, then got serious again.

"As the team choreographer, I say we stick to the original plan," Taylor said. "Amy's the flyer."

"It's up to Sadie, not you," Amy argued.

"And me," Lindsey said. "Cheer club was my idea."

"Hmm." Taylor pursed her lips. "I thought it was Sadie's."

She was right. But on Sadie's growing list of things-the-Pack-has-to-agree-on, "who invented Cheerleading Club" was at the bottom.

"We came up with it at the same time, right, Sadie Lady?"

"Ummm . . ." Sadie began scratching her head, pretending to be distracted by a fake bug that was fake caught in her ombré hair. Spineless? Perhaps. But she needed a moment to think.

If Amy was afraid to fly, Sadie didn't want to push her. But at the same time, Taylor was right. Amy was the lightest and, therefore, the best one for the job. As the leader, it was Sadie's responsibility to make the call. But whose side was she supposed to take? How was she supposed to trust her instincts when she had no idea which instinct to follow?

It was times like these that Sadie questioned the magic carousel. What if it glitched? What if she wasn't a lion-light? What if she was a timid mouse instead?

"I'll be the flyer," Sadie offered. Broken bones would be less painful than another minute of this argument.

"How does that make sense? You and Lindsey are the strongest ones here. You're natural-born basers."

Lindsey cut a quick look to Taylor, those fierce, emerald-green eyes pointing at the solution.

"Do you want to be our flyer?" Sadie asked Taylor.

"Fine. Let's start with an open pike basket."

Amy removed a pair of glasses from her yellow fanny pack and slid them on. "Let's start with something easier."

"Nah, we've got this," Sadie said, hoping she was right.

After Taylor explained the technique (several times!), they gathered on the mattresses and created what looked like a woven basket with their hands.

Taylor stepped on. "Don't forget to catch me when I land."

She wobbled a little, then began counting them in.

"Ah-five, six, seh-vun, eigh—"

With a sharp thrust of their arms, Sadie, Lindsey, and Amy hoisted her into the charcoal-gray yonder.

"What thaaaa—" Taylor shouted.

If she said more than that, no one heard her. They couldn't see her either. The girl was gone.

"Where is she?" Sadie asked.

"Saturn," Lindsey said, as if it were a good thing.

Amy pressed her glasses firmly against the bridge of her nose and squinted into the darkness. "This is why I didn't want to be the flyer."

"Taylor!" Sadie called, heart pounding. "Tayyyy-lor!" She removed her hands from the basket bind. "What have we done?"

"Relax, cat," Lindsey purred. "She's just scared."

Reminding Sadie that chameleons camouflage when they're scared *was* helpful. But it didn't change the fact that it had been almost ten seconds, and Taylor was still gone.

Then they heard, "Incomiiiiing!"

"Where are you?" Amy shouted at the sky. "We can't see—"

"Hands in basket!" Taylor yelled, her voice getting louder. "Nowwwww!"

The girls quickly joined hands.

"My arm was on top." (Lindsey.)

"No, mine was." (Sadie.)

"Does it matter?" (Amy.)

"Move to the left!" (Taylor.)

The girls shuffled.

"OTHER LEFT!"

"We can't see you!" Sadie shouted. "Where are—"

A sudden force, bearing the crushing weight of Mount Kilimanjaro (had the 19,000-foot African mountain taken flight and then fallen from the sky) knocked them all to the mattress. Winded and stunned, they landed facedown in a limp heap.

Soon, fingers wiggled and legs twitched.

"That was awesome!" Lindsey said. Then she began to laugh the kind of laugh that usually ends with sobbing. "And look"—she lifted her hands—"my claws are puuurfect! Not a single chip."

Ideally, the others would have found the whole thing awesome, too. Before long, they'd all be quaking and rolling around in hysterics. A real *you-had-to-be-there* bonding moment they'd treasure for life. But this was not an ideal world. Not even close.

"We need to do that during the actual game," Lindsey pressed. "The fans will love it!"

"Um, hello, are you serious?" Taylor asked, struggling to stand. "You just shot me through the ozone layer! Climate change is on you."

"I think my cranium is broken," Amy moaned.

"If we used our powers," Lindsey said, ignoring their pain, "people would come from all over the world to watch us cheer. SpaceX would name a rocket after us. Kids would dress up like us on Halloween!"

"And we'd be locked in cages at IBS," Sadie added.

"Cowardly lion," Lindsey growled.

Sadie ignored the jab because Lindsey was right. Sadie was afraid. Afraid of IBS, afraid of getting kicked out of Charm House, and afraid of putting her Pack in harm's way. She was also tired of asking Lindsey to hide her truth from the world. Lindsey wasn't wrong for taking pride in her gifts. The world was wrong for making her hide them. And that was too much to think about before breakfast.

"Let's work on our squad name," she suggested. It *was* Tuesday. The Allendale coach would be evaluating their routine on Saturday, and so far, a near-death experience was all they had to show for it. "Any ideas?"

"The Charm House Cheerleaders," Amy said.

Lindsey quickly pointed out that they were cheering for Allendale, not Charm House. "What about the Party Animals?"

"Um, hello, that has nothing to do with cheering," Taylor said.

"Okay, um, hi, then how about Spirit Animals?"

"We can't," Amy said, the sky starting to lighten, along with their moods. "It's cultural appropriation."

They looked at her sideways.

"That's when you take on elements of a culture that's not your own." Amy removed her glasses and returned them to her pouch. "*Spirit animal* is a Native American term that—"

Lindsey yawned. "What about AnimalX! Like SpaceX, only—"

"We should probably avoid the word *animal*," Sadie told them. "We don't want anyone to think we're—"

"What? Different? Powerful? Special?" Lindsey stood and began pacing. "I'm so over being told we should be ashamed of—"

"What about the Pack?" Sadie offered, trying to keep things upbeat. "It says animal, without being obvious."

"Yeah." Taylor cocked her head. "But should it be more footbally?"

"What about QuarterPack?"

"Or LinePacker?" (Amy.)

"Or RunningPack?" (Taylor.)

"Or FullPack?" (Sadie.)

"Or BackPack?" (Lindsey.)

They all started laughing. *Finally!*

"What about Packman?" (Taylor.)

"Ms. Packman." (Amy.)

"Pack a Lunch." (Taylor.)

"Nick Knack Patty Pack." (Amy.)

"Heart Apack." (Lindsey.)

"Pack and the Beanstalk." (Sadie.)

"Step on a Crack, Break Your Mama's Pack." (Amy.)

"Wait!" Taylor said. "Do squads even have names? Don't they have the same name as the team they're cheering for?"

Sadie sighed. "I think you're right."

At some point, the sun had risen and the birds started chirping. The breakfast gong would sound shortly, and they hadn't made any progress. They didn't have a routine, a uniform, cheers, or glitter. "Let's move on."

"Who cares if squads don't have names? We can start a new trend," Lindsey said. "I don't want to be a Cougar, do you?"

"No, but we don't want to attract attention either, remember?" Taylor said.

"Attracting attention is literally the whole point of cheer-leading!"

The breakfast gong rang. "We don't have time to argue about this," Sadie insisted. "Can we please just move on?"

And so they did.

They moved on to breakfast, to a full day of classes, and bedtime. Then they moved on to Wednesday morning and Wednesday at dinner.

In.

Total.

Silence.

Their squad had zero cheer, and Sadie had two days to find it. This cat may have *had* nine lives, but she was down to what felt like her very last one.

ten

On Wednesday evening, after an awkwardly silent dinner with the Pack, Sadie ditched her leonine pride and slid a note under Lindsey and Taylor's dorm room door. Then she did the same for Amy. It read:

> *I want to say I'm really sorry,*
> *For being bossy and getting roar-y.*
> *Having fun is my only goal,*
> *Let's meet up at the Watering Hole.*
> *We'll soak in the tub and make things right,*
> *I'll listen to your ideas; I promise not to bite.*
> *Our club will rule, everyone will applaud,*
> *2-4-6-8 Gooooo, Squad!*

On the off chance that apology poems work, Sadie hurried to the Watering Hole, anxious to greet her friends when they arrived.

Friends. That word lingered as she padded across the slippery spa tiles on her way to the soaking tubs. She had *friends.* Yes, they were experiencing a bit of tension, but tension was a good thing, according to Sadie's mother. Feeling *something,* even when that thing is negative, shows you care. It's when you don't feel anything, not even anger, that the relationship is over. "The opposite of love isn't hate," Lori always said. "It's indifference." Sadie didn't know much about her mysterious powers or her three unusual pack mates, but she was sure about one thing: She had never cared about anything more in her life.

To prove it, she slowly lowered herself into the Lava tub. (Once the girls arrived and admired her sacrifice, she'd high-tail it to the Arctic tub with Lindsey.) Its scalding heat was meant for cold-bloods like Amy and Taylor, not girls who melt ice cream sundaes with the touch of a spoon. And yet, there she was—jaw clenched and eyes tearing as the boiling water ravaged her skin and made her fingers swell. At least Beak's ring was safe.

One she acclimated, Sadie closed her eyes, inhaled the eucalyptus-scented steam, and wondered how much of the "tension" was her fault. What would an experienced lion-light have done?

According to one of the many articles Sadie googled on leadership, her job was to consider everyone's ideas and choose the one that best suited her brand. And in this case, her brand was about *not* standing out and *not* getting noticed.

The Allendale coach was the only person she needed to impress. With a feuding pack, no routine, no uniform, and two days left, that wasn't going to be easy. But there she was, tail between her legs and soaking herself dizzy. Lindsey was right. If only they could use their powers . . .

The door pumped open. Feet began slapping against the tiles. Sadie sat up and gave way to her burgeoning smile. *They came!*

With faces impossible to distinguish in the milky steam, three girls walked arm in arm toward the Easter tub. It was really called the Red Sea because the temperature was warm but not boiling. But Kate, Amy's former roommate, was a wannabe spy with a soft spot for secret codes and disguised certain words by saying them backward. So when she changed the Red Sea to Aes Der, the girls said it sounded like Easter and went with it.

"Can we please do Lava today?" Unfortunately, it was Aubrey, the bony lizard-light, who rolled her ankle during her dance performance on Family Day.

"Nurse Walker said Arctic only until the swelling goes down," said Rachel. The monkey-light was shouldering Aubrey as she limped through the mist like a war-torn zombie.

"The swelling *is* down," Aubrey insisted.

"Yeah, it used to look like a cantaloupe. Now it looks like a grapefruit," said Lizzy, the monkey-light on her other side. "It's supposed to look like an ankle."

Must be nice, Sadie thought as she lifted herself to sit on the lip of the tub before she passed out. Would she ever feel supported by her friends again? She checked her Trkr app, hoping Beak might cheer her up. He was at football practice.

Just then, a familiar voice called, "You in there, Lady?" It didn't sound angry at all.

Sadie quickly lowered back into the cauldron. "I'm in Lava," she said, fanning her flushing cheeks.

"Yes!" Amy and Taylor called at the same time. They slipped in with ease while Lindsey stood above them, tiger-striped robe tied tightly around her waist.

"We're so glad you apologized," Taylor said before dunking her head.

"Seriously?" Amy said, flutter-kicking. "That whole silent thing felt like trying not to look at the sun during a solar eclipse. Of course, you can't, so you want to, even more, you know?"

"Major meows on the poem, by the way," Lindsey purred.

"Agreed," Taylor said, emerging. "It's hard to admit when you're wrong." She rested her chilly hand on Sadie's bicep. The cold came as a delightful shock. The lack of accountability was also shocking. Minus the delightful part. Was it the dehydration talking, or did they not owe her a few *we're sorry too*s?

"Gotta hit the cat box," Lindsey said, excusing herself.

The sound of clanging glass followed her into the bathroom but was gone when she returned.

"What *was* that?" Sadie asked.

"What was what?"

Sadie lifted herself out of the tub. "Did you have elixir vials in your robe pocket?" she whispered.

Lindsey rolled her eyes. "I don't know what you're talking about." Then she leaned closer to Sadie and whispered, "I hide them in my robe pocket and flush them." She punctuated the confession with a wink as if they were on the same side of this rebellion.

They were not.

"Linds, you need to be taking that."

"Why?"

"To get your memory back."

"It doesn't help," Lindsey insisted. "I remember more when I don't take it."

Sadie began scratching her arms. Lying was itchy. "That's impossible."

"No, it's not," Taylor said from the tub. "You should have heard what happened today in Instinct Control."

"I was there," Sadie said. "You just pretended I wasn't."

"Oh yeah," Taylor giggled.

"Remember when Professor Jo told us about the boy she took to the hospital?" Lindsey said as she lowered down beside her. "How he was bleeding so much she fainted?"

Sadie nodded. Of course she remembered. She also knew

what Professor Jo didn't tell the students: that Beak was the random boy. He had been in a coffee shop with Lindsey when a teenage girl cut the line. The girl denied it. So Lindsey, who was still in public school and hadn't yet learned to control her animal instincts, launched a full-scale tiger attack. When Beak pulled his sister off the innocent stranger, she accidentally clawed his cheek.

"So?" Sadie said with a dismissive shrug. "Professor Jo made up some random story to teach us about empathy. Who cares?"

"That's the thing," Lindsey said, green eyes shining like headlights in the steam. "I don't think she made it up. I think it actually happened and I feel like . . ." She leaned even closer and exhaled. "I feel like I was there."

"Same," Sadie lied. "The story was very descriptive."

Lindsey drew back her head. "Um, hi. No, it wasn't. Professor Jo said she took a bleeding boy to the hospital and fainted because she empathized with his pain. That's it. But I knew the bleeding boy was at Froth Coffee. I knew that the teenage girl was hiding behind the counter, crying. And I knew there was another girl—" Lindsey squeezed her eyes shut and began rubbing her forehead. "I can't see her, but I can *feel* her . . . It's like I *was* her. I felt her fear and her shame. Like maybe I was the reason the boy got hurt."

Nauseated, Sadie sat on the damp tiles, hung her head

between her legs, and inhaled the soothing scent of eucalyptus. It didn't help. "Why would you be the reason?" she asked the way Ruth, her old therapist, might have.

"No clue," Lindsey said. "But I'm going to find out."

"How?"

"For one, I'm ditching my elixir. Whenever I stop taking it, my memory—"

"Bad idea," Sadie interrupted.

"Why?" Taylor stepped out of the tub. "Don't you want Lindsey to remember her parents?"

"'Course I do." It didn't matter that her Pack surrounded her. In that moment, Sadie had never felt more alone. As long as Sadie knew the truth about Lindsey and had to pretend she didn't, *lonely* would be her default setting.

"If you want Lindsey to find out who her parents are, why are you telling her to take that elixir?" Taylor asked, working her wet hair back into spikes.

Oh, the irony! Taylor, the Czar of Safety, was literally leading Lindsey into danger.

"Tay, is that you?" Aubrey called.

Taylor's ears perked up. "Aubs?"

"Hey, Tay!" said Rachel and Lizzy.

Taylor padded closer to the Arctic tub and shivered. "What are you doing in there?"

Aubrey sighed. "Nurse Walker said the swelling has to go down before I can dance."

"Dance? Does that mean you're going back to the Flash Lights?" Taylor asked, mostly curious. However, there was something else in her tone. It was sharp and maybe even a little bitter. Like dark chocolate trying to pass for sweet.

"She has to," Rachel teased. "You ditched us."

Taylor opened her mouth as if to defend herself but didn't speak. What could she possibly say? She *did* ditch the Flash Lights. But not for just anyone—for her pack mates. Which is where Taylor should have been all along.

"Rachel's kidding," Lizzy said with a nervous giggle. The monkey-light knew better than to antagonize a Pack member. "We miss you. That's all she's saying."

Taylor lowered her eyes and sighed. "Yeah."

"Okay!" Sadie said with a clap of her hands. It was time to get down to business.

"We need to talk about—"

"The memory I had?" Lindsey said.

Sadie giggled as if Lindsey was joking. "You mean the thing you imagined?"

Lindsey stood and tightened her robe. "I don't get it. It's like you *want* me to forget."

"No, it's not," Sadie said, unable to meet Lindsey's gaze.

"Yes. It. Is." She looked to the others for backup. Taylor nodded in agreement. Amy was still in the tub, texting. "Amy!"

Amy quickly lowered her phone and turned it face-down. "What?"

"You agree, right?"

"Yes!" Amy said. "With what?"

"That Sadie's acting like she doesn't want me to remember anything."

"Uh . . ." Amy cocked her head. "I wouldn't say *anything*. More like *some* things."

Lindsey lifted the gold nail file around her neck and began pushing back her cuticles. "Well, you did say that, actually. On our way over here."

Sadie stood. "You were talking about me?"

"For a few minutes, yes," Lindsey said, refusing to apologize. "But then we moved on."

"Moving on sounds great," Sadie said. "Can we please work on our club?"

"Sure." Amy stepped out of the tub and wrapped herself in a plush towel. "When?"

"Uh, now?"

"I have a tutoring appointment in ten minutes."

"Who are you tutoring?"

Amy's cheeks flushed pink. "Don't remember. I have to check. I just know I have someone at eight o'clock."

Sadie looked to Taylor. "We can still figure out the routine, right?"

"I can't. I have to dye my hair purple for tomorrow," Taylor said.

"Why? What's tomorrow?"

"Uh, Thursday?"

"I know it's Thurs—" Sadie stopped herself midsentence. The girls had to be messing with her. She quickly scanned the room for hidden cameras. Maybe she was being filmed for a prank show. All she saw was steam.

"What about you, Linds? We can design our uniforms, pick the music, work on our—"

Lindsey shook her head and pointed at her temples. "Throbbing."

If you took your elixir, your head would feel better, Sadie wanted to shout, along with things like, *Amy, you can recite all 118 elements in the periodic table. How do you not remember who you're tutoring? Taylor, you're prioritizing dyeing your hair purple? Really?* And *This club is the fastest, easiest way to get my grades up. Without it, I will have to leave Charm House. Why doesn't anyone care?*

But Sadie didn't want to push them away any more than she already had. Instead, she chose more silence.

eleven

Sadie stuffed a binder full of team-building exercises into her backpack, added a deck of cards, four blindfolds, pens, a stack of paper, matches, and Red Vines because the secret candy cupboard in the teacher's lounge was out of Twizzlers.

Holding the zipper's pull, she considered dragging it closed slowly, one tooth at a time, the way she always did when Amy was sleeping. But it was five a.m. and Sadie needed Amy awake. So she let the zip rip.

Despite the sudden noise, Amy remained asleep, the orange light from her heat lamp warming her like a rotisserie chicken.

Sadie flicked on the light. "Wakey, wakey, little snakey!"

Amy pulled the blankets over her head.

Sadie yanked them down.

Amy covered her face in pillows.

Sadie shut off the heat lamp.

Amy shot up. Her topknot flopped forward.

"Nice unicorn-horn," Sadie said.

"What are you doing?" Amy collapsed onto her stack of pillows. "What time is it?"

"Cheer Camp time!"

"Huh?"

"Come on!" Sadie urged, pulling Amy back up. "I was awake all night planning."

"Planning what?"

"Fun ways to bond."

"Bond? We're literally a Pack."

"In life, yes, but not in cheer," Sadie insisted. "We have to work better as a team and I figured out how." She gave Amy a stack of warm clothes. "Come on!"

Yes, Amy was half asleep and fully irritated but she would perk up after she played Sadie's team-building games. They all would. And if not . . .

Sadie slung the backpack over her shoulder and shook the thought from her head. If not was so not an option.

Inside Lindsey and Taylor's room, the sound of chirping crickets, croaking frogs, and thunderclaps blasted from Lindsey's sleep machine. The ultraviolet rays from Taylor's mood-enhancing light turned the pink shag rug purple and the white stripes on the zebra wallpaper blue. *#Terrariumgoals*

"Welcome to the Glow-N-Bowl!" Sadie bellowed. "Home of the nacho-scented rental shoes!" She smiled a little, expecting a laugh.

She got crickets, frogs, and thunderclaps.

Granted, hers wasn't the *best* impersonation of Loud Lou, but anyone who had ever been to a glow-in-the-dark bowling birthday party in Timor Lake (which was everyone) knew who she was referencing.

"Two-four-six-nine, Cheer Camp's starting, rise, and shine!" Sadie announced. "It's time to make like James and bond! Be like a fund and trust! Act like a tree and—"

"Leave," Taylor mumbled, purple spikes of hair poking out of her blankets.

"I was thinking *root*, but leaf kind of works," Sadie said, even though it didn't.

"I said leave, not leaf."

Amy yawned, then slipped into Taylor's bed. "Why do you always want to practice in the middle of the night? Is it a nocturnal thing?"

"It's not night. It's five o'clock in the morning, and no, it's not because I'm nocturnal. It's because—" Sadie was about to say *This is the only time everyone is available.* But instead, she said, "It's a surprise!"

Sadie lifted Lindsey's satin blindfold and removed her foam earplugs. "Come on, Linds, please," she said, wishing she didn't sound so desperate. "It will be fun."

"Why are you doing this?"

"For our cheer squad."

Lindsey lowered her blindfold.

"Who's Archie Guad?" Taylor mumbled.

Sadie rolled her eyes. Was she seriously serious right now? "Our cheer squad! You know, pom-poms, Allendale Cougars, future road trips, memories."

"Oh, right." Taylor rolled onto her stomach.

"Come on. Get up! I've planned fun games and sketched out some uniform ideas. Once we all agree on something, I'll ask Gia and Jasmine to help us make them." Sadie turned off the sleep machine. "Oh, and I have prizes."

"Give us a few minutes," Taylor muttered.

"How many?"

"Two hundred and forty," Amy said.

They began giggling into their pillows. Sadie felt their shaking laughter in the depths of her stomach. Couldn't they see how hard she was trying?

Sadie turned toward the door, defeated. Did she really think her team-building exercises, prizes, and uniform sketches would be enough? Because they weren't. And neither was she.

"Wait!" Amy called. "Two-four-six-nine, can't we pick another time?"

"Two-four-six-one, how about when class is done?" Taylor said.

"Two-four-six-two, don't you all have stuff to do?" (Sadie.)

"Two-four-six-forty, we'll make this practice a priority." (Amy.)

"Two-four-six-nine, that won't give us very much time." (Sadie.)

"Two-four-six-um, hello?" Lindsey said. "It's not like we have any competition, so don't stress, cat. I'm going back to sleep. We'll do this after school." She turned on her sleep machine.

The conversation was over.

twelve

*T*he cheer audition was thirteen minutes away and the girls were . . . well, Sadie didn't know where they were. She *did* know they weren't in the barn with her, fine-tuning their routine for Coach Sterling, and she was stress pacing herself dizzy.

Desperate for a distraction, Sadie FaceTimed Beak. She had planned to tell him about the squad *after* it was official, but her look wasn't just on point, it *was* the point. Her mane was glossy, her black-striped claws were refreshed, and the bronze bodysuit she'd borrowed from Lindsey accentuated her muscles—muscles Sadie usually kept hidden. She wanted Beak to see her before the audition sweat kicked in and wilted her wow.

Two-four-six-eight, check me out, I look great!

She casually placed a fingernail by her mouth and waited for him to answer. And waited. And waited. It was Saturday morning. Where was he? The Trkr app placed him in his dorm room. But was he really sleeping at 11:55 a.m.? Or was he ignoring her call? They hadn't been able to connect in days. Maybe he'd moved on. The thought made Sadie bite down on her perfect nail.

"Don't gnaw the claw!" Lindsey shouted as she entered the barn. If she was sorry for being late, she certainly didn't look it. Her tiger-striped hair swayed merrily; her smile was smug and entitled.

"Hey," Beak said, finally picking up. Sadie declined the call. "Where were you?"

"I had to *you-know-what* in the *you-know-what*."

"No, what?"

Lindsey leaned close and, in an almost silent, cats-only tone, muttered, "I had to flush another vial of elixir down the toilet."

"You did not!"

Lindsey beamed. "Did too."

A sudden wave of nausea forced Sadie to sit. When was the last time Lindsey drank her elixir? How long until she figured out the truth? Weeks? Days? Minutes? She should have told Miss Flora the moment she found out Lindsey was fake-taking. But Sadie couldn't rat out her pack mate. They had a pledge.

Sadie was about to bite down on her fingernail when Lindsey smacked her hand.

"Pause on the claws in your jaws." She pulled Sadie up to stand. "It makes you look nervous, and you have nothing to be nervous about. No one will be at this audition but us. Zero pressure."

"You can say that again," Amy said as she hurried toward them, dressed to sled. "I tried to warm up with a hot shower and there was, like, no water pressure. Just a light trickle. It felt like hugging a crier." Shivering, she reached under her puffy jacket and got the moisturizing oil from her fanny pack. "My scales are starting to scale."

"Yeah," Taylor said. "My fingers feel like frozen fish sticks."

"*Taylor?*" Sadie scanned the barn. The chairs from Family Day had been removed, the stage dismantled. Bales of hay had been stacked along the walls to block the windows. Nothing but an empty stretch of straw-dusted earth lay before her. "Where are you? When did you get here?"

"Been here the whole time." She slid the scarf off of Amy's neck and draped it over her camouflaged body. "See?"

Sadie thought of her mother's living-room lamps. How Lori would hang a sarong over the shades to soften the light when she entertained. "What's with the camo-mode?"

"Stage fright," Taylor said.

"But there's no stage."

"And no pressure," Lindsey reminded them.

"Trigger alert!" Amy said, still upset about her weak shower.

"The toilets in the Watering Hole aren't flushing either," Taylor said.

Sadie cut a look to Lindsey. *The vials!*

Oblivious to the implication, Lindsey began swiping her lips with gloss.

". . . And this is the barn," Miss Flora said as if concluding a tour. She was with a bald man wearing navy joggers and a red tank top that promoted *Blood. Sweat. Respect.* He had the kind of wide shoulders that made one assume the rest of him would be wide, too, but he narrowed at the torso like a capital *T.*

"So you weren't joking?" he scoffed. "You really don't have a gym?"

Miss Flora removed her glasses and let them dangle from the chain around her neck. "There are two things you should know, Coach Sterling. First, Charm House girls exercise in nature."

"Admirable," he said, somewhat delighted. "And the other?"

"I never joke."

"Taylor, they're here," Sadie whispered. "Show yourself."

"It's hard for me to appear under pressure."

"Trigger alert!" Amy hissed. "Stop talking about pressure."

Sadie quickly removed Amy's scarf from Taylor's body and nudged her toward the barn door. "Go outside and come back when you're visible. We'll cover for you."

Taylor ran off, marking the earth with her footprints as she went.

"Welcome, Coach Sterling," Sadie called, her right arm extended for a handshake as she hurried to cover Taylor's tracks. "Thank you so much for coming."

He walked toward her with matched enthusiasm, his feet slightly splayed, like a duck's.

After a round of introductions, he said, "I'm a little embarrassed I didn't think of having a squad sooner."

"You didn't think of it," Lindsey said. "I did."

Coach Sterling laughed, assuming Lindsey was joking.

"I like this one," he said to Miss Flora. "She's full of fight."

Miss Flora grimaced. "You have no idea."

He clapped his hands together, then quickly rubbed them back and forth. "Should we get going or wait for the other squad?"

"Oh, it's not another squad. It's just one more person. Taylor. She just ran to get something. She'll be right back."

Coach Sterling turned to Miss Flora. "I thought you said two squads were trying out."

"I did. Cackle. They should be here any minute."

Cackle? Sadie's ears began to ring, and yet, she could hear the clangor of Amy's and Lindsey's pounding hearts. She quickly side-eyed Miss Flora. Could she hear their panic, too?

The headmistress raised a knowing eyebrow and slid on her glasses. Her expression hung somewhere between contempt and delight.

"Cackle, huh?" Coach Sterling jutted out his bottom lip

and nodded. "I like it. Sounds like crackle. Which makes me think of fireworks. Which makes me think of winning. Which makes me think of trophies. Which makes me think of wanting that coaching job at Ohio State."

Amy began slathering her arms in oil. "I didn't know they were trying out."

"None of us did," Lindsey said. "How did they even know about it?"

"I imagine Sadie spread the word as I asked her to," Miss Flora said.

Sadie just stood there, unsure of how to respond. She didn't spread. So who did?

Then her phone began to chirp. It was the sound effect she assigned to Beak's contact. Chirping birds to compliment his nickname. His adorable picture—seven-year-old Beak dressed as a black-eyed boxer for Halloween—gave her a zing. Still, she tapped the screen and declined the call (again!).

"That ring you're wearing!" Lindsey said when she saw Sadie's thumb. "I know it."

"It's Beak's. I told you, he asked me to hold it for him during practice and—"

"And the guy in that picture," Lindsey said, pointing at Sadie's screen. "I know him too."

Sadie's skin began to prickle. "Because it was Beak!"

"No, I knew him *then*. Like, when that picture was actually taken. He used a Sharpie to color his eye black, and he couldn't get it off for weeks and—" Lindsey grabbed the sides of her head and doubled over in pain.

Miss Flora shot Sadie a fiery look of contempt as she rushed to her granddaughter's side. Before she could say anything, Cackle entered the barn, chanting:

"Navy, navy, and red, Cougars gonna put you to bed! Navy, navy, and red, Cougars gonna get in your head! Navy, navy, and red, Cougars gonna knock you dead!"

They entered in a spirited but straight line dressed in the Allendale school colors—navy pleated miniskirts, red unitards, and matching pom-poms that they waved around their annoyingly energetic bodies. They had all the pep and promise of a box of Skittles. While the Pack just stood there stunned, like a sticky clump of raisins.

"Well, this is exciting!" Coach Sterling said. "We have a real showdown. A fight to the finish. A—"

"My brain!" Lindsey cried.

"She's fine," Sadie managed. "She just needs air. We'll be right back."

Sadie and Amy took Lindsey by the arm and led her outside.

Miss Flora was about to follow them when her phone rang.

Thoughts swirling, Sadie hurried past Cackle, intent on avoiding their triumphant grins.

"How did they find out about the auditions?" Taylor asked when they convened on the side yard of the barn.

"No clue," Sadie said.

"Where did they get those uniforms?" Amy asked while rubbing orange oil over her arms.

"No clue."

"How do I know that kid in the picture?" Lindsey asked weakly.

"No clue. All I know is we need to get it together. Taylor, get visible. Amy, wipe that oil off your arms so we can hold a basket grip without slipping—"

Amy giggled. "You mean a basket *slip*."

Sadie was too stressed to smile. "And, Lindsey, forget about that picture and get in the zone—"

She was interrupted by a voice over the loudspeaker. "A pipe has burst in the Watering Hole. The school is flooding. Students and staff must evacuate the building and gather on the back lawn for roll call. This is mandatory. I repeat, mandatory . . ."

"The pipes?" Miss Flora said into her cell phone as she hurried from the barn. "I don't understand how this happened . . . Did you call Kelvin? . . . An hour? . . . How vile . . ."

It certainly was. About ten vials, to be exact. But Lindsey didn't seem to make the connection. Instead, she padded toward the lawn with the others, rubbing her temples and muttering softly to herself. And Sadie, who should have been concerned about Lindsey's returning memory, Taylor's stage fright, Amy's scaling body, and Cackle's competition, walked beside her with a satisfied grin. The Pack needed a second chance with Coach Sterling, and thanks to Lindsey's royal flush, they had one.

thirteen

Outside Sadie's dorm room window, the bruise-colored sky was dumping rain. But inside was even more depressing. Amy was in the chemistry lab working on a venom that would paralyze her victims for ten minutes. Taylor was practicing "camo control"—the ability to camouflage even when she wasn't in danger—and Lindsey was in a tree house napping. Sunday funday? More like Sunday un-day.

A visit to the Den for advice on how to handle, well, everything that went down at yesterday's cheer audition would have been Sadie's next move. But the Watering Hole was off-limits while a team of plumbers and whoever else deals with broken-pipe messes tried to clean things up. Why Lindsey flushed the vials along with the elixir was a real mane-scratcher. It's like she was trying to mess things up. Which she did. Sadly, studying for Monday's Scent Identification test was Sadie's only plan.

"Quiz me," she told Amy as they sat down to breakfast the following day. She handed over her note cards, then folded a piece of bacon into her mouth. A whoosh of joy shot from her toes to the top of her head. Mainly because the chef had cooked the bacon to crispy perfection, but also because she was prepared for this test. Like, really prepared. Sadie knew all twenty-five scents and the human emotions each one represented. She was going to get a perfect score and her parents would let her stay.

"When people are sneaky," Amy read, "they smell like blank."

Sadie's hand slammed down on the table like a game show contestant hitting a buzzer. "Cackle smells like chlorine and brown sugar."

"Correct." Amy flipped to the next card. "Sardines and chocolate smell like . . ."

"Fear. As in, I will smell sardines and chocolate when we hunt them Cackle and make them pay for crashing our audition."

"Okaaay. Uh, the smell of pencil eraser and cat pee indicates blank."

"It indicates danger. Which is what Cackle will smell when I get revenge on them."

"Wow," Amy scoffed.

"Why *wow*?"

"Um, hello. You're kind of obsessed with revenge, don't you think?"

Sadie drew back her head. "Aren't *you*?"

Amy opened her mouth to answer but stopped when Cackle passed by their table. The smell of sardines and chocolate dominated. Eyes forward, Liv and Val hurried by, clearly afraid of a confrontation. But not Mia. Maintaining an average pace, she angled her head ever so slightly and glanced at Amy. Amy glanced ever so slightly back. The exchange was so quick Sadie would have told herself she imagined it, but she could hear Amy's heart beating double time. She was hiding something, and Sadie knew what it was. During one of their tutoring sessions, Amy must have told Mia about their secret cheer audition. The snake sssspilled.

Amy anxiously flipped to the next card. "Let's keep going . . ."

Sadie correctly identified each scent, and Amy congratulated her with a cold-handed high five.

"Perfection!" Amy beamed. She popped a hard-boiled egg in her mouth and swallowed it without chewing—something she did when nervous.

Miss Finkle, cafeteria monitor and all-knowing owl-light, swooped in and gripped Amy by the shoulder. "Use your teeth, Miss Rogers."

Amy's shoulders slumped forward. "Sorry, ma'am. I forgot."

Meanwhile, Sadie sat up taller than ever. She was going to get a perfect score on her test—goodbye, pressure, and hello, not-having-to-get-homeschooled-by-her-mother.

Taylor slid her green breakfast tray next to Sadie's and sat down. "Sorry I'm late," she said, smelling like a wet puppy. *Exhaustion.* "I was up half the night and couldn't get out of bed." Her Mohawk had not been groomed to standard. What had once been a robust row of purple peaks was now a sad, windblown valley.

"Let me guess," Sadie tried. "You were plotting revenge on Cackle."

"No, Lindsey."

"You were plotting revenge on Lindsey?"

"No, she was talking in her sleep. At least, I think she was sleeping. I'm not sure. Can tiger-lights file their nails and sleep at the same time?"

"Lindsey probably can," Amy said while cutting a hard-boiled egg into bite-sized pieces.

"What was she saying?" Sadie asked. The smell of salted lime filled the air. It was concern—her own.

Taylor looked up at the arched ceiling and squinted as if the answers were hidden in the stained glass. "She said, 'I think I knew you when you were younger,' and 'Have you ever been to Froth Coffee?' and 'If you lie to me, I'll scratch your—'"

Sadie pushed her tray aside. Her appetite was suddenly gone. "This is bad!"

"Too crispy?" Taylor asked.

"No, this Lindsey thing."

Taylor and Amy looked back at her in a way that reminded Sadie of her old dog, Kit-Kat. Gaze fixed and expectant, sure that a treat was on the way. In this case, the treat was the truth—the real reason why Lindsey was saying those things and who she was planning on saying them to. But Sadie couldn't feed that treat to them. Could she?

Miss Flora, Professor Jo, and Beak swore her to secrecy. And yet, this was about more than keeping secrets. It was about Lindsey's safety. Maybe even Beak's. Her mother always said, "Never tell on someone to get them in trouble. Only tell to get them out of trouble." And instinct told Sadie that Lindsey was in trouble.

"Lindsey is not okay."

"I know," Taylor said. "She had a terrible headache this morning. She went to see Nurse Walker."

"Are you sure that's where she went?"

Taylor blinked. "Where else would she be?"

Sadie opened her mouth to speak but nothing came out. It was as if her voice were giving her one last chance to reconsider. But she couldn't. The weight of her lies was too heavy to carry alone.

"Lindsey's elixir is made of Amy's venom," she blurted.

"Huh?" Taylor blink-blinked. "What does that have to do with anything?"

"Everything."

"The venom Miss Flora drains from me every day?" Amy asked. "She's using it on Lindsey?"

Sadie nodded. "Miss Flora isn't draining it because you make too much. That's a lie. She's using it for an elixir that blocks Lindsey's memory."

"Why would she block Lindsey's memory if she wants Lindsey to remember?"

Sadie sighed. *Here goes . . .* "She doesn't. That's the point. She doesn't want Lindsey to know who her parents are."

Taylor laughed as if Sadie might be joking. "That's impossible," she said. "Miss Flora *wants* Lindsey to remember. She's trying to help."

Sadie shook her head. "She thinks if Lindsey knows who her family is, she'll rebel even more than she already has."

"Why?" Amy asked. "Who are they?"

Sadie paused. Answering that would reveal the bigger secret, the one that would destroy her relationship with Miss Flora and possibly get her kicked out of Charm House whether her grades improve or not. And not answering? Ha! The girls knew Sadie knew.

There was no turning back.

"GrandmotherMissFloramotherProfessorJobrotherBeak," Sadie quickly said. She felt lighter. Then she felt heavier.

Taylor ran a hand through her hair. "There's no way!"

"Way!"

"Impossible."

"Possible."

"How long have you known?"

Sadie crinkled her nose apologetically. "A bit."

"And you didn't tell us?"

"I couldn't! I promised Miss Flora."

"What about the promise you made to Lindsey?" Amy asked.

"Shhhh," Sadie begged. "Keep your voice—"

"What about our Pack pledge?" Taylor pressed. "You know, where we swore we'd be honest and true?"

Sadie gripped her roiling stomach. "I was trying to keep her safe. We all were."

"How is not telling her who her parents are keeping her safe?"

"If she doesn't know who her family is, she'll think twice before running away, and if she knows who her dad is, she'll probably attack—"

"Wait." Taylor stiffened. "Who's her dad?"

Sadie lowered her head onto the table and muttered, "Karl Van der Beak. The head of IBS."

Taylor and Amy began talking at the same time, though Sadie could barely hear what they were saying over the ringing in her ears. What had she done? Miss Flora was going to destroy every one of her nine lives. Then kill her again.

"You have to tell Lindsey the truth," Taylor insisted.

Sadie lifted her head. It felt like the cafeteria was spinning—a kaleidoscope of safari-beige uniforms, stained glass, and green trays. "I'm afraid she already knows. She's been fake-taking her elixir and her memory is coming back. We have to find her."

The gong rang. Breakfast was over. It was time for class.

"I'm sure you'll see her in Scent Identification," Amy said, her tone sharp and frosty. "You have a test, right? Or were you lying about that, too?"

"I wasn't lying," Sadie tried. "I was trying to protect—"

Amy and Taylor got up, left their trays on the table, and hurried for the doors. Not even pretending to wait for Sadie, who was left behind to clean up their mess.

"Take your seats," Professor Olga insisted as she ushered the students inside.

Sadie stopped at the door. There was no sign of Lindsey. No trace of her rose and leather scent. She was gone. Had she busted into Miss Flora's office, claws drawn and ready to fight? Was she on her way to confront her father at IBS? What if her headaches were so bad she'd collapsed?

How could she enter the classroom like everything was normal when Lindsey could be in danger? At the same time, how could she *not*? Professor Olga was handing out the test.

A test Sadie had studied for. A test she needed to ace and knew she would.

Just then, her phone chirped. It was Beak. She sent him to voice mail and searched the hallway. *Where is Lindsey?*

Beak called again.

Sadie sent him to voice mail again.

He called.

She sent.

He called.

She sent.

Then a text appeared on her screen. It read: SHE'S HERE. NEED HELP. NOW!!!

Instead of fighting or fleeing, Sadie froze, paralyzed by the heft of this colossal decision. If she went, she'd save Lindsey. If she stayed, she'd save herself.

She considered telling Professor Olga what was happening, but that would only make things worse. Sadie was a lion, a leader. She had to handle this on her own.

fourteen

Milky bands of sunlight winked between the trees as Sadie ran toward Allendale.

Light.

Dark.

Light.

Dark.

Light.

Dark.

She felt like she was running in a movie theater as the feature presentation flickered across the screen. If she was to have any hopes of a happy ending, she needed to move faster. But while her mind was wanting action-adventure, her legs were all drama and folded beneath her. Lions were like summer-camp crushes. They were powerful but couldn't endure long distances.

Sadie stopped to catch her breath and checked her Trkr app in search of Beak's location. First, it said that he was inside Allendale. Now he was heading outside. Was Lindsey still with him? Was she about to scratch a C-shaped scar on his other cheek? Had she unleashed her inner tiger? Was IBS on their way?

Sadie texted Taylor and Amy, asking them—*begging* them—to tell Professor Olga she had a rancid case of food poisoning and couldn't take the test. She stared at her phone, waiting for a response that never came.

They were obviously mad at her for keeping that secret. But you know what? Sadie was mad at them for being mad at her.

What was she supposed to do? Betray Miss Flora? Betray Beak? Put Lindsey in danger? Sadie had been put in an impossible situation. Why couldn't they understand?

Sadie found Beak and Lindsey on one of Allendale's tennis courts. She was on one side of the net, and he was on the other. Every time he circled to her side, she circled to his.

"Linds!" Sadie called as she hurried toward her. "You're safe!"

"Leave me alone!"

"I'm not going to hurt you," Sadie said as she approached. "I just want to talk to you."

"I'm done talking. I want answers. Can you give me answers?"

"I don't know what answers you're looking for," Sadie lied.

"Yeah, I didn't think so." She began walking backward, widening the gap between Sadie and herself.

"Why are you doing this?" Sadie pleaded. "It's not safe."

"Nothing is safe," Lindsey fired back. "And *he* has something to do with it." She pointed at Beak, who was pacing on the other side of the net.

"You're safe for now, but you won't be if you don't come back to Charm House."

"It's not a house—it's a prison!" Lindsey insisted.

"Come on, Linds! We have to go." Sadie took three steps forward.

Lindsey took four steps back.

Sadie stepped forward.

Lindsey ran for the fence and made it over to the other side with a single pounce.

"Wait!" Beak called after her. But it was too late. She hopped up the trunk of a nearby tree and refused to come down.

"What *happened*?" Sadie asked him as they made their way toward her.

Beak ran a hand through his black hair and sighed, as if exhaling for the first time in hours. "She stormed into the dining hall during breakfast, ate the sausages off my plate, and told me to tell her who her parents are."

"Did you?" Sadie mouthed, assuming Lindsey could hear them.

Beak shook his head. "Luckily, Link, Colter, and I got her out of the dining hall before the teachers noticed. But you have to get her back to Charm House, Sadie. She's in danger."

Sadie, now at the tree, squinting against the midmorning

sun, glimpsed wisps of Lindsey's tiger-striped hair blowing around her face. Angry, in a tangle of branches, Lindsey looked like she was posing for a perfume ad.

"Let's go! Please," Sadie pleaded.

"Where?" Lindsey shouted from the leafy beyond. "*Harm House*? Never. The answers I need are out here and I'm going to find them."

"Well, they're not in a tree, I can promise you that," Sadie tried. "Come down and I'll help you look."

"Ew. No. You come up."

Nice try, Sadie thought. Lindsey knew she was a tragic climber. She couldn't even make it up to the tree houses behind the school. And that was back when Sadie had nubby baby-carrot fingers. Now she had long, manicured claws. She couldn't possibly grip stick without breakage. But she had to prove her loyalty, personify courage, save the day. BE A LION! Especially since Beak was watching.

Sadie petted the tree's bark as if that would make a difference. *Be a nice plant and let me climb you, okay?* She wrapped her arms around the trunk, hoping her lion-light magic would kick in and whisk her up like an elevator. No such luck.

Maybe she was overthinking it. Maybe she needed to take action. Like in the movies. What would Gal Godot do? Scratch that. Gal would use cables and special effects, maybe even a stunt double. The real question was: What would Wonder Woman do?

Sadie took a few steps back and dashed toward the tree. She leapt at the last moment and wedged the tip of her sneaker into a groove in the bark.

I did it! she thought. *I did it!* But she was only about a foot higher than she was before. There was a long way to go.

"What are you doing?" Beak asked, sounding adorably perplexed.

"Warming up." Sadie reached for another groove. *I can do this! I can do this!* But when she tried to lift herself, she lost her grip and fell to the ground with a thud. *Thanks for the extra weight, bacon!*

While Sadie wiped the mud off her uniform, Beak hovered, emerald eyes hard and impatient. The bubbly soda mist feeling Sadie usually felt when she was around him flattened to tap water. The unfiltered kind that gave people dysentery.

Where were Amy and Taylor? She closed her eyes and tried to channel the Whisper's soothing voice but heard Lindsey's instead.

"You don't get it," Lindsey said. "You have Lori and Dean. I don't have anyone. I mean, I *didn't* have anyone and now I might so—"

"Pause! Just because I know who my parents are doesn't mean I don't get it," Sadie said. "I bounced like a tennis ball between their houses for ten years. At school everyone either ignored me, called me Hairy Poppins, or wrote Sa-DIE on my locker. So believe me, I get the whole feeling-alone thing.

But none of those things matter anymore. Charm House is my home now. You're my family, and I'm yours."

Sadie could hear Lindsey's racing heart slow to a light jog. It was working!

"Come down and let's figure this out. Together," Sadie said, wishing someone, at some point, had said that to her. "I'd come up there, but gravity is obsessed with me and won't let me go." She held up her hand and crooked her fingers. "Claws, Paws, and Jaws," Sadie said, and began to recite the Pack pact. "I pledge my soul to the Charm House Pack. I will be honest, true, and have your back . . ."

She shot Beak a look. *It's working. I've got this.*

Hands in pockets, he began walking toward the school, backward. Watching like the overprotective brother he was forced to be.

"These stripes on my nails are an eternal vow. To be fierce, to be loyal, to be the cat's meow . . . ," Sadie continued.

Lindsey wasn't joining in, but one of her gold-and-black bejeweled Vans appeared below the tree's leafy canopy. *Finally!* She was climbing down.

"No matter what happens, no matter the cause . . . ," Lindsey said.

The more they recited, the more Lindsey appeared until her whole gorgeous self was hugging the tree trunk and shimmying down.

Sadie did it! She'd followed her instincts, and it worked!

Lindsey landed on the ground, looked deep into Sadie's eyes, and said, "I think I knew Beak when I was younger. Like, really knew him."

"You did!" Sadie said, forgetting again what she was allowed to say and what she wasn't.

"Huh?"

Oops.

"I mean . . ." A prickly woosh of heat gathered under Sadie's armpits. Was she supposed to be in loyal-friend mode or do-the-right-thing mode? Why weren't they the same modes? She didn't know anymore. Her brain hurt. Her heart ached. And Beak was glaring at her in the distance. She could feel his anxiety in her belly. Feel his ire on her skin. "What I mean is, I believe you."

Lindsey folded her arms across her chest and angled her ear toward Sadie's thumping heart. "You're lying, lion. I hear your heart."

"I'm not lying. I *do* believe you."

"You believe I knew Beak when he was younger? You don't think I'm making it up?"

"I know for a fact you're not!"

"Wait, what?" Lindsey said. "How?"

The smell of sardines and chocolate was strong. Sadie didn't have to turn around to know that Beak was behind her. "What are you doing?" he muttered.

The world stopped spinning on its axis. Or at least it felt

like it had because Sadie began to wobble. She wanted to turn it back and reverse time. "I mean . . . I . . . um . . ."

"What do you know? What aren't you telling me?"

"Nothing," Sadie tried. But her voice was soft and her conviction softer. There were too many lies. Their cumulative weight was impossible to carry and even harder to speak.

Lindsey stood there, hands on her hips, waiting for an explanation. When one didn't come, she began to run. "You know what, forget it. I don't trust either one of you. I'll find the answers myself."

"Wait!" Beak called. "Where are you going?"

Lindsey ran faster.

Sadie wanted to chase her but couldn't. She was paralyzed by shame.

"Get her!" Beak shouted.

Vision blurring with tears, Sadie took off. Even though she could clock 200 meters in twenty seconds, Lindsey got a head start. There was no way to catch her.

Then, *bam!* Lindsey tripped and landed on a leafy mound of dirt. Before Sadie could figure out the cause of her good fortune, Taylor's foot began to appear. Her triumphant smile quickly followed.

"Have a nice trip, see you next fall," she said as she became visible.

"Nice camo control!" Sadie beamed.

Lindsey began pushing herself up to stand. "What the—"

"Hold her down!" Amy said as she emerged from the bushes. "I've got this!"

Despite Lindsey's thrashing, Sadie got her back onto the ground and Taylor contained her arms.

"Get offa me!" Lindsey roared. She began bucking and writhing, doing whatever she could to break free. Whatever Amy was going to do, she needed to do it now.

"Hurry!" Sadie called.

Like the slithery snake-light she was, Amy shot from the bushes, fangs bared, and bit down on Lindsey's arm.

"Owie!" Lindsey shouted. "Did you seriously just—" Her eyes fluttered closed, and she was still, heart purring like a kitten sitting poolside.

"Thank you," Sadie sighed, holding her friend's limp body.

"We didn't do this for *you*." Taylor stood. "We did it for Lindsey."

"Because she's a *real* pack mate," Amy was quick to add.

"You're one to talk," Sadie snapped.

"What's that supposed to mean?"

"It's your fault Cackle auditioned for cheer."

"How is that Amy's fault?" Taylor asked.

"She told Mia we were trying out."

Amy's gray eyes widened. "Why would I do that?"

Sadie listened to Amy's heartbeat. It was speeding, not hammering. She was angry, but not lying. "Then how did the hyenas know about our audition?"

"No clue. Ask *them*!" Amy said, turning her back on Sadie and linking her oily arm through Taylor's. "Let's go, *friend*."

"Whatever you say, *friend*," Taylor responded as the pair skipped back to Charm House as if they were off to see the wizard.

Only then did she notice that Beak was gone, too.

The weight of one hundred elephant-lights pressed upon Sadie's chest. Not only was Sadie failing Scent Identification, but she was also failing life.

Lindsey's gold bangles clanged as Sadie lifted her off the ground and cradled her like a gigantic newborn. *Here we go again.* Forget Claw Spa and her cheer squad. Sadie could start a Venom Victims Club dedicated to carrying passed out people through the woods. First Amy, then Beak, now Lindsey . . .

As Charm House came into view, Sadie found herself agreeing with her mother. Homeschool was the only school that made sense. Sadie wasn't a good leader. She wasn't even a good follower. She was a lion-light who couldn't climb a tree, keep a secret, or make long-lasting friends. It was time to confess everything to Miss Flora and let the big cat take over. Then Sadie could go back to her room and lick her wounds until her parents picked her up and took her to the only place she ever belonged.

By herself.

fifteen

Miss Flora was standing at the entrance of Charm House, as stiff as her silver bob.

She already knows.

But how?

Sadie approached her slowly, carrying Lindsey like a protective shield. If she didn't rest her Jell-O-ing limbs, she was going to melt into a puddle right there and ruin Miss Flora's kitten heels.

"She's okay," Sadie assured Miss Flora as she extracted Lindsey from her arms. If the dead weight of Lindsey's muscular body was too heavy for the old lion-light, she certainly didn't show it. With little effort, Miss Flora slid her arms under Lindsey's torso and cradled her like a newborn.

"*This* looks okay to you?" she hissed.

Sadie opened her mouth to answer. A creaky-door sound came out instead. What was she expected to say? What was she supposed to hide? Oh, wait. She was going to confess everything, right? *Ugh!* The voices inside her head were so loud she couldn't hear herself think.

"Beak called me," Miss Flora said.

Sadie's mouth went dry. "What did he say?"

"Everything." Miss Flora gently laid her granddaughter on the fresh-cut grass. "We're going away for a while and we're taking Lindsey with us."

"Where are you going?"

Miss Flora scoffed. "You expect *me* to trust *you* with that information?" Her gaze was fixed on the distant mountain ranges. "Those days are over, Miss Samson."

A sudden pang inside Sadie's belly caught Sadie off guard. Instead of food, she craved sympathy. She was not a bad person. Miss Flora didn't understand. No one did. "I was trying to help. I swear."

"If you wanted to help, you would have come to me the moment you realized Lindsey had stopped taking her elixir. Or the moment you knew she wasn't at breakfast. Or the moment Beak told you where she was. At Allendale. Instead, you skipped a test, took matters into your own hands, left campus, and exposed our family secret." Her tone was void of color, her message black and white. "Now get to class. I'll deal with you later."

Suddenly, a flashy red Mustang raced up the driveway and spun to a stop. A pounding bass line blasted from its open windows. When the engine was cut, Professor Jo opened the driver's door and planted her worn combat boots on the asphalt. Her choppy platinum-blond hair spiked like a dog's hackles. Not only could Professor Jo break a man's wrist easier than a toddler could snap a stick of celery, but she could also spot a rabbit from a mile away and jump twenty feet in the air. But with that hot rod? Now she could reach 0 to 60 mph in 5.1 seconds, and judging by the harried look on her face, the eagle-light was ready to fly.

"Let's go, Mom." Her hazel eyes went straight to Miss Flora as if Sadie weren't even there.

If Professor Jo had been giving out gold stars for Instinct Control, Sadie would have received an entire constellation. There she was, standing perfectly still, even though she wanted to plead her case, beg for forgiveness, cry. Instead, she tried to remember what she'd learned about controlling her instincts through single-pointed focus meditation, how it calmed the mind. So she concentrated on the diamond stud in Professor Jo's beaklike nose and how it glinted in the sun. But then her beak reminded Sadie of Beak's beak and her focus scattered like dandelion fluff.

If she could just run back to Allendale and explain her side of the story, Beak would understand that Sadie hadn't meant to betray anyone's trust or put Lindsey in danger. She'd been trying to save her. Then Beak would take her back and—

Professor Jo whistled sharply, a sound so piercing Sadie felt it in her gums.

Then the passenger door of the Mustang opened, and a navy-blue Converse stepped onto the asphalt. Then another. An effervescent tingle bloomed deep inside Sadie's belly. She didn't have to race back to Allendale. Beak was here!

"Hey!" she said at the sight of him. He brushed by her, went straight for Lindsey, and attempted to lift his sister's limp body.

"Let me help," Sadie said.

"Ha!"

"Beak, please, I feel so bad about this. Let me—"

"This isn't about how *you* feel, Sadie," he grunted as he struggled to get Lindsey into the car.

It was harsh, but maybe Sadie deserved it. Maybe this *was* her fault.

"When will you be back?" Sadie asked as Beak slid his sister onto the back seat. She could hear the regret in her voice.

Instead of answering, Beak lifted his phone and tapped the screen. One second later, Sadie heard a ding. There was a new notification on her Trkr app. It read: BEAK STOPPED SHARING HIS LOCATION.

"Seriously?" Sadie asked.

Beak emerged from the Mustang and Sadie's insides soared with hope.

"Can we just talk?" she asked, chin trembling.

He stepped toward her and held out his hand. *A peace offering!*

When she reached for it, Beak stepped back and opened his palm. "The ring," he said. "Can I have it?"

His request landed like a punch to the gut. Still, Sadie managed to twist the gold band off her thumb and release it. "You're mad at me for telling the secret and Taylor and Amy are mad at me for *not* telling the secret. I couldn't win either way. How is that fair?"

"This isn't about fair, Sadie," Miss Flora interrupted. "It's not about winning, loyalty, or friendship. It's about making unpopular decisions to keep you girls safe. I thought I made that clear when I invited you into our inner circle."

With that, Miss Flora, Professor Jo, and Beak got into the car and slammed their doors.

Vision blurring with tears, she watched as the Mustang pulled a one-eighty and sped through the iron gates, a cloud of dust billowing behind them.

Alone and afraid, Sadie lifted her gaze to the Virgin Mary statue above the entrance, the one with the missing arm, and began to sob. Not only for herself, but for the statue, Lindsey, and everything else in her life that was broken.

sixteen

*S*adie wasn't about to roll into second period twenty minutes late, eyes swollen and red, with pieces of her broken heart falling around her feet like shattered glass. And she certainly wasn't going to seek refuge in her room. What if she ran into Amy? Sadie had had enough trauma for one day, thank you very much.

The Den was her only option.

She dipped her toe in the tranquil stream, fearing the silky water wouldn't transform into colorful sand this time. With her luck, wiggly eels or stinky sardine guts would appear instead. Something that reflected her life. Fortunately, the water turned grainy at her touch, and the face of the rock slid open.

Sadie paused at the entrance, expecting to be greeted by the soothing *Welcome to the Den* voice, but heard nothing. Great. The Whisper was giving her the silent treatment, too.

Then *whoosh.*

The fire ignited when she stepped inside, painting the walls with licks of flickering gold. Wishing she had been wearing one of her old sweatshirts instead of her Charm House uniform, Sadie reached for a hood that wasn't there. Her hot blood ran cold.

"Hello?" she called. "Is anyone here?"

Silence.

Maybe she should have called before stopping by. Her mother always said it was the polite thing to do. But who would she call? Besides, the last time she popped by the Den, the Whisper was there and happy to advise. No warning necessary.

Sadie sat by the fire and waited.

And waited.

And waited.

She couldn't help thinking of her glow-in-the-dark bowling birthday party. How no one showed up except her grandmother, who then beat her by forty points and ate her French fries. Or the time she waited in the lab for her science partner so they could work on their movement-of-tectonic-plates-using-s'mores project. Her partner never showed, and the s'mores hardened. Now this.

And all because Sadie was worried about Lindsey, tired of carrying her family's secret, and sick of lying to her friends. All because she needed someone to say, "I understand why you kept the secret and I understand why you shared it." Even if that "someone" was a whisper.

But there was no one.

Sadie left the Den and dialed her mother.

And dialed.

And dialed.

It was useless. The Watering Hole was a dead zone. If Sadie wanted reception, she'd have to step into the hallway and risk being seen by, well, everyone.

Instinct (and hunger) led Sadie to the caf, where she paced outside the doors and tried her mother again. Not even the wafting smell of ground beef could distract her. She wanted out.

Thankfully, her mother picked up on the first ring. "Hello? Sadie?" Lori said, breathless. There was communal *om*ing and birdlike *cawing* in the background. "Is everything okay?"

"What's that sound? Did you get a parakeet?"

The lunch gong rang, and the classroom doors flew open. Chattering girls woke the halls as they made their way to the caf.

"Did I get a what?"

"A PARAKEET!" Sadie shouted as Kara and Sondra approached.

"Makes more sense than a lion," Kara muttered to Sondra, as if Sadie weren't standing right there.

Sadie covered the phone. "What's that supposed to mean?" she asked.

They brushed by her without answering. Which was fine.

Sadie already knew. Parakeets were big talkers and clearly so were Amy and Taylor. They must have told Sondra and Kara about the big betrayal. And if they told Sondra and Kara, they told everyone.

"Sadie, are you still there?"

"Yeah, uh—" She paused as the hyenas approached, sniffing and yipping, circling. She was vulnerable without Lindsey, and they knew it. "Get away from me!" Sadie pushed past them with such force that Liv and Val slammed into the stone wall.

"What's going on?" her mother pressed. "Are you okay?"

"Bad reception. Hold on." Sadie hurried into the stairwell. "You were right. I need to be homeschooled. Like, now. Will you pick me up?"

"Did something happen?"

"It's the classes. They're too hard," Sadie lied. But it was better than telling her the truth—that she skipped her Scent Identification test to save Lindsey, that her bad grades just went from bad to worse. Her mother, like everyone else who mattered, would never understand. "So can you come?"

"I'm on a yoga retreat in Joshua Tree, sweetie. I won't be back until Sunday."

"That's, like, six sleeps from now," Sadie said, aware of the panic in her voice. If the hyenas didn't get her by then, the isolation would. "What about Dad?"

Her mother scoffed. "Camping with his poker buddies."

"Can you *please* come get me now? I'll never ask you for anything ever again."

"I don't have a car. I carpooled with Gardenia." She took a sharp inhale, held it, then exhaled slowly. "Sunday is the earliest I can be there," she breathed. "Okay?"

No. It absolutely was not okay. It was the opposite of okay. It was yako. The hunter had become the hunted, and there was nowhere to hide.

seventeen

Sadie drew a big, red X with her Sharpie in the "Friday" box of her *Punny Sayings* wall calendar, one of the few things she had left to pack. This month's illustration was of an annoyingly smug kitten saying "Pawsitivity is key!"

She yanked it off the wall.

The worst week ever was almost over. Amy had been sleeping in Taylor's room and had taken her heat lamp and oils with her. The hyenas were still yip-yapping about their successful cheer audition and were more power-hungry than ever. She could hear them sniffing outside her door, conspiring to shave her mane and swipe her food until she was too weak to fight. Without Lindsey there to protect her, without *anyone* there to protect her, the cat was a sitting duck.

Lindsey . . .

Everyone thought Sadie knew where Miss Flora and Professor Jo had taken her and that Lindsey's absence was Sadie's fault. It didn't matter how many times she tried to explain herself, they called her "the lying lion."

Thirty six hours to go . . .

Sadie slipped her calendar into the sleeve of her suitcase, zipped it shut, and took in her dorm room. Empty. Just like her.

The following morning, the sun burned through the milky haze like a promise. It was a day for optimists and crushes. Friends and Frisbees. Long lunches and laughter. Everything she didn't have but desperately wanted. At least she had bacon. A huge plate of it, which she took to the back lawn to avoid the predators.

Dewy grass licked the sides of her feet as she flip-flopped to the base of the tree houses. Each flip seemed to say *fraidy,* each flop said *cat. Fraidy-cat. Fraidy-cat. Fraidy-cat . . .* The faster she walked, the more insistent the mocking became, every rubber slap a new punch to her pride.

Once Sadie finished eating, she'd climb one of the ladders and hide out for the rest of the day. Maybe the fresh air would lift her sagging spirits. Probably not.

Just as she was taking her first bite of bacon, the school doors pumped opened. Dozens of girls spilled onto the lawn, food trays and picnic blankets in hand. It was a glorious fall day, one of the last they'd have before the rainy season, but eating outside? They rarely did that. Were they coming for Sadie? Taking advantage of Miss Flora's absence? *Both?*

Everything made sense when Cackle took center field. They had been wearing their red unitards and pleated navy miniskirts all week, to which they had recently added a dizzying number of sequins.

As everyone settled onto their blankets, Liv connected her phone to a portable speaker and blasted "My Head & My Heart" by Ava Max. Cackle began rustling their pom-poms and high-kicking for the whooting audience. Sadie zeroed in on Mia—the *nice* one. Or at least the less threatening one. And yet, her welcoming full-moon face was now eclipsed by a cold, standoffish glare when she met Sadie's eyes.

Still, she envied their synchronicity. Their spirit. Their bond. All Sadie had was a hood, which she cinched tightly around her head.

"Excuse me, sir," said a girl. Her voice was high-pitched and piercing. Like she had just inhaled a balloon full of helium.

Sadie looked up and squinted.

"I'm Gleesa," she said, as if that was supposed to mean something.

Sadie removed her hood, hoping to embarrass Gleesa for thinking she was a boy, but the woman's over-bronzed cheeks didn't blush. Her glitter-dusted eyelids didn't blink.

Her strawberry-blond ponytail didn't wag. She just stood there, hands on her narrow hips, toothy as a Colgate model, smiling for a camera that wasn't there.

"Can I help you?" Sadie asked.

"Coach Sterling sent me. I'm the spirit pumper."

Sadie shielded her eyes from the glare of Gleesa's teeth and said, "The *what*?"

"I help new cheer squads get a leg up." She giggled. "Pun intended."

"Sorry, I don't really know what you mean."

Gleesa sighed. Her breath smelled like spearmint. "I was hired by Coach Sterling to get Cackle ready for next weekend's homecoming game." She pointed at the glittering girls high-kicking on the field. "Is that—"

Sadie nodded.

"Yikes," she said, and began bouncing toward center field.

Sadie inched a little closer and gathered her hair behind her ears to eavesdrop. Gleesa could have been there to spirit-pump the Pack. Gleesa *should* have been there to spirit-pump the Pack, and Sadie wanted to know what she was missing in a misery-loves-more-misery sort of way.

After a quick round of introductions, Gleesa asked Cackle to show her what they had.

Liv cued up her music.

"No music," Gleesa insisted. "I want to hear your cheers!"

On the count of three, they shouted:

Snap, Cackle, Pop,
Your team is gonna drop.

"You can't be serious."

"We can and we are," Val said. "Why?"

"This is about Allendale, not Cackle. Your cheers have to be about them."

"And you call yourself a feminist?" Mia said.

"No, I call myself a spirit pumper."

"Why would we cheer for Allendale?" Mia pressed. "They're not cheering for us."

"They're not supposed to!"

"Exactly. Which is why we have to cheer for ourselves."

"Yeah," Liv added. "If we don't, who will?"

"The *fans,*" Gleesa said, handing them a packet of papers. "These are the approved cheers. There are sixty of them. Thirty for home games, thirty for away games. Memorize them all." She clapped her hands. "So where's the rest of your squad? I want to see your base, evaluate the flyers, and prep your advanced loads."

"Ali Crawford took an advanced load this morning," Val said, pinching her nose. The girls doubled over laughing.

"Seriously," Gleesa said. "Where's the rest of your squad?"

"This is it," Mia said.

"You're joking, right?"

"We never joke," Liv joked.

"This isn't a squad," Gleesa huffed. "It's not even a *quad*. We need a minimum of fifteen. Oh, and what are you doing for uniforms?"

Val cocked her head. "What's wrong with these?"

"Nothing, if you want to blind the players."

A few of the onlookers giggled nervously as Cackle exchanged a look. Not even they could find the humor.

"Are you girls serious about cheer?"

"Is anyone?" Val asked.

"Why did you even try out for Coach Sterling?"

Liv shrugged. "We wanted to beat the Pack."

"I have no idea what that means but—" Gleesa's phone rang. "Speak of the devil." She cleared her throat and summoned that toothy smile of hers. "Hello, Coach . . . Yes, I'm here . . . No. No, it's not . . . Welp, it's an attitude thing . . . and a skill thing . . . and a . . . Sorry, can you hear me now? Great . . . Bottom line? They're like a bunch of wild animals . . . not cheer material . . . I already thought of that . . . There's a spunky dance troupe at St. Margaret's who . . . Seriously?" She began pacing. "How about now? . . . Now? . . . Ugh!" She jiggled the phone. "Dang *Wi-Fi*!"

Val flashed a mischievous grin, then pointed at one of the tree houses. "Up there."

Gleesa thanked her with a sharp nod, told the coach she'd call him right back, and began climbing. Moments later she called down, "It's still not working!" as if they were responsible for her wireless connection.

"Keep trying," Val called. Then she kicked the ladder away.

"Hey, what are you doing? Put that back!"

"Why did the cheerleader bring a ladder to the restaurant?" Liv shouted.

"Why?" Mia asked.

"Someone told her the food was on the house!"

Everyone laughed except Gleesa, who threatened to call the police if they didn't get her down.

"You and whose cell service?"

Gleesa waved her phone like a deadly weapon. "You don't need cell service to call nine-one-one!"

"Maybe that troupe from St. Margaret's can help you!" Val called as Cackle began making their way back to school, ladder in hand. "Let's go!" she told the spectators. Everyone packed up and followed.

Sadie stood. "You guys! Wait! Bring the ladder back!"

They kept walking.

"That's it!" Gleesa shouted after them. "I'm dialing!"

Sadie quickly caught up with Cackle. This was about more than power, more than control. It was about keeping the police away from Charm House and protecting its students. "Come on! This is serious!"

"So are your split ends," Mia said.

"What happened to you?" Sadie asked. "You used to be kind of nice."

She thought she saw a glimmer of humanity in Mia's eyes, but it was quickly gone. "What can I say? I have multiple personalities. And they all think you're a bad friend."

"Put the ladder back," Sadie growled.

"No!" they growled louder.

Fine. If they weren't going to do it, Sadie would. She grabbed a splintering rung and yanked it toward her. The three girls yanked harder.

"Let go," Sadie said, pulling again. "I know you don't like her, but you have to control your instincts or she's going to tell on you."

"Who is she going to tell?" Val barked. "Professor Jo? Miss Flora? You got rid of them, remember?"

"I did not!" Sadie said with a definitive yank. One that should have sent the girls flying into the forest, but they were holding so tight, the weather-worn ladder split in half.

"Ooopsie." Liv smirked.

"Hello, police?" Gleesa said, loud enough for everyone to hear. "I'm calling from—"

"Hang up!" Sadie yelled. "I'm coming to get you!"

Val laughed. "A lion who can't climb a tree is going to save the cheerless cheerleader. This is gonna be good."

Ignoring them, Sadie ran toward the tree, grabbed hold of the trunk, tried pulling herself up, and fell. Her black-striped nails were too long to grip the bark. She tried again and failed again. The sound of laughter swirled around her. Her first instinct was to run. Not back to school, not into the woods, but past the iron gates and as far away from these beasts as possible. Her second instinct, the one she was usually too angry to listen to, reminded her that she was a lion-light and that she would always be a lion-light, whether anyone believed in her or not. And her third instinct? That one said, *These nails have got to go.*

Before Sadie could change her mind, she bit them and spit them. She didn't need the black stripes anyway. The Pack was done.

Heart pumping like a piston, she took a few steps back and ran toward the tree. This time she wasn't thinking about failing or succeeding. She wasn't thinking about status or bragging rights. She had one singular mission. To keep Gleesa from bringing the authorities to their campus. With that in mind, she leapt onto the bark and pawed to the top in two effortless hops.

"Impressive." Gleesa beamed, lowering her phone.

"Get on my back."

"Wait, what? No, dude! You can't *carry* me down!"

"I'm not a dude and yes, I can."

When they reached the bottom safely, no one applauded. No one high-fived her. No one congratulated her for making it to the top for the very first time. Everyone was gone.

"Whoa, your strength is incredible," Gleesa said, tightening her ponytail. "Have you ever tried out for cheer?"

If she only knew.

"You'd make a killer base and a great captain for my new squad."

"New squad? What about St. Margaret's?"

"Yeah, no. I kind of fibbed about that. They're a high school troupe. No way would they cheer for middle."

"Oh." Sadie's eyes drifted to the ladders leaning against the other trees. Why didn't she think of that? At that same time, she was glad she didn't.

"What do you say?" Gleesa asked. "Be my base?"

"That's very nice of you," Sadie told her, "but I'm leaving Charm House tomorrow."

"Where are you going?"

"Homeschool."

"Can't say I blame you." Gleesa hooked her bag over her shoulder and surveyed the empty lawn. "If you change your mind, let me know."

"I will," Sadie said. But there was only one squad that she wanted to be part of and they didn't want anything to do with her.

eighteen

Sadie was back in her room playing solitaire, cheating just to keep things interesting.

On the other side of her locked door, the hyena-lights were loping back from the Watering Hole, entertaining yet another group of girls with a play-by-play of how they trapped Gleesa in a tree house.

"I can't believe you left her there," Kara, the dingo-light, gushed. "That's so bold."

"That's what happens when you raise Cackle's hackles," Val warned.

Liv and Mia yipped with delight. They didn't care that their cheerleading days were over. Destroying the Pack and gaining power had been their mission and they'd accomplished it in spades.

Spades . . .

Sadie needed the king of spades to complete her sequence. She drew a four of hearts instead and decided to start a new game. If only life were that easy.

Distracted by the rumbling *vroom* of a car engine, she hurried to the window. Professor Jo's Mustang was rolling through the iron gates. They were back!

Sadie's first instinct was to run outside and hug Lindsey breathless. In this scenario, Lindsey would hug her back. Through tears of joy, they'd notice that neither one of them had removed their Cat's Claw friendship necklaces and that would make them cry harder. Sadie would start to apologize, but Professor Jo and Miss Flora would beat her to it. After begging for Sadie's forgiveness, they'd thank her for forcing them to get honest with Lindsey. Then Beak would emerge from the car with a bouquet of daisies (how did he know?) in one hand and a gold ring on the other. The same as his. While sliding it onto Sadie's thumb, he'd promise never to question her intentions again and—

The loudspeakers crackled. "Good afternoon, Charm House students," Miss Flora said, as if she had been there the whole time. "Please report to the barn at three o'clock for a mandatory assembly."

Sadie stepped away from the window and returned to her cards. The voices in the hall turned to frenzied whispers and wild predictions about the nature of this impromptu gathering.

"That's twenty-nine minutes from now, girls!" Miss Flora urged. "Tardiness will not be accepted."

Feet scurried and doors slammed. Then came a knock.

"Sadie, open up!"

Amy!

It had been a week since Sadie heard Amy speak her name, speak to her at all. It sounded foreign and felt fantastic. The Pack had been treating Sadie like she was invisible, but this proved that she hadn't fully disappeared.

"Be right there!" Sadie unlocked the door, fueled by hope. If she could just explain . . .

"I need my cloak," Amy said, brushing past her.

Oh.

Sadie returned to her bed, wondering if Amy noticed the suitcases—how they were full and their room was empty. Or if she even cared. If she had, she didn't show it. Amy went directly to her closet, pulled out her cloak, and slipped it over her purple sweats.

When she realized Sadie was watching, she turned her back and muttered, "Are you just going to sit there?"

"What am I supposed to do?"

"Get your cloak and go to the barn."

"I'm leaving Charm House tomorrow." Sadie's chest tightened. It was the first time she'd said it out loud. "So there's no point."

Amy stopped fussing with her cloak but didn't say a word. She just stood there. Still and silent. "I told you I'd tutor you."

"I'm not leaving because of my grades," Sadie said. "I'm leaving because I think Charm House will be better off without me."

Amy turned to face her but remained silent, her gray eyes wide and hungry. Was she taking in Sadie's words? Swallowing them whole like one of her hard-boiled eggs?

"I made a mess of everything and I'm sorry," Sadie continued. "Maybe I should have told you and Taylor what was going on. Maybe I should have told Lindsey, too. But Miss Flora asked me not to and—" She sat on the edge of her bed. The springs creaked and sighed. "I was trying to do the right thing, I swear. But you're right. Pack mates shouldn't keep secrets from each other."

Sadie exhaled. She had said her piece and expected Amy to leave, but she didn't. Instead, she reached under her cloak, unzipped her yellow fanny pack, and removed her body oil. "You're not the only one who kept a secret."

"What do you mean?"

Amy began massaging the oil into her scaling skin. "It's about Mia. I know you think I was tutoring her . . ."

"You weren't?"

"I was. Kind of. In the beginning, but then . . . it was more than that." Amy's heart began beating rapidly.

"What do you mean by *more*?"

"Like"—Amy blushed—"more, more."

"More, more?"

"More, more."

"Oh," Sadie said as this new information washed over her and refreshed her outlook. Amy had a crush on Mia. "Does she more-more you back?"

Amy's heart beat even faster. "Yes." Then she lifted her chin and struck a pose. "Can you blame her?"

Sadie giggled. "Why didn't you tell me?"

"There was too much species rivalry," she said, chin lowering. "I was afraid. We both were."

Sadie's chest tightened again. For Amy's pain this time.

"The tutoring kind of brought us together again and . . . well . . . we kind of kissed." She smiled shyly, exposing her two fang-like teeth. It felt like years since Sadie had seen them. *Hello, old friends!*

"Amy, that's great!"

Amy's fangs disappeared as her smile faded. "You really think so?"

"Why wouldn't I?"

"Because . . . you guys said spending time with Mia was a conflict of interest. Taylor used those exact words. Which is why I haven't told her yet. I haven't told anyone."

"You told me," Sadie said, proud of being the first. It was a good sign, right? "And you *know* I can keep a secret."

"True." Amy grinned. Then she lowered her head in her hands and muttered, "It sucks."

"What sucks?"

"Not being able to tell your best friends about one of the biggest moments of your life?"

Sadie thought of her tree triumph. "I get it."

"Not that it matters. Mia and I ended it."

"Why?"

"Because . . ." Amy began tugging a loose thread on her cloak. "I didn't want to choose between her and you guys."

Sadie's heart broke a little. It was bad enough that animal-lights had to hide behind the iron gates of Charm House. Hide from IBS. Hide their true potential. But hiding from friends was the worst kind of hiding ever. "Amy, you shouldn't have to choose."

"Then why did you make me?"

Ouch.

"I didn't mean to . . ."

"Well, you did. So did Lindsey and Taylor and Val and Liv. You all did."

"Is that why you told Mia about the cheerleading tryouts?" Sadie asked. "Because you liked her?"

Amy's gray eyes narrowed. "I didn't tell Mia! I would never do that!"

"But if you didn't, then how—"

"Cackle heard you and Lindsey talking about it outside Miss Flora's office. Mia tried to stop them, but they didn't listen. She had our backs."

"Not anymore," Sadie said with certainty.

"Well, she *did*. Until she realized you guys were the reason we couldn't hang out."

So that's why Mia was acting so mean. "I really messed things up, didn't I?" Sadie said.

Amy shrugged. "We both did . . . It takes two to tangle, right?"

"I think it's tango."

"Yeah, but I don't dance. I'm too clumsy." Amy adjusted her cloak. "My tangos look like tangles."

They both smiled a little. It was a warm smile, heated by fond memories and undeniable love. Then Amy cooled. "Are you really leaving tomorrow?"

"I am," Sadie said, bracing herself for Amy's begging. But Amy didn't beg. She simply lifted her hood and turned toward the door. "Taylor and I will be sitting in the back if you change your mind."

"So that's it? You're just going to leave?"

"It's not me who's leaving," Amy said. And then she was gone.

In the hallway, students hurried toward the stairwell, exchanging theories about Miss Flora's agenda. Once they cleared out and the silence returned, Sadie heard another sound. Something familiar. A waterfall burbling in the distance.

The Den was calling her.

It, too, was ready to say goodbye.

nineteen

"**W**elcome to the Den, Sadie," the Whisper said in its familiar hushed tone. "Come in."

The flames from the smokeless fire were already dancing, reflecting orange licks of light on the cave walls. It knew she would come.

Sadie settled onto the heap of pillows, and the door closed. *Goodbye, smokeless fire.*

"It's good to see you, Miss Samson."

Sadie wasn't in the mood for pleasantries. What was the point? "I needed you on Monday and you weren't here."

"And yet, you survived."

Sadie scoffed. "Barely."

"Are you saying that nothing good happened this week? Nothing at all?"

Sadie thought about her failed Scent Identification test, being shut out by the Pack, Beak blocking her on Trkr then asking for his ring back, that Miss Flora and Professor Jo no longer trusted her, Lindsey's absence . . . "Nothing at all." She glanced down at her fidgeting hands, her bitten nails, and remembered one thing. "Oh, I climbed my first tree."

Goodbye, first tree.

"That's something!"

"I guess." Sadie could have told the Whisper how she rescued Gleesa and smoothed things over with Amy, but tomorrow those "good things" would be one of many memories she'd push aside and try to forget.

Goodbye, fellow animal-lights.

Goodbye, dances in the clearing.

Goodbye, Paws, Claws, and Jaws.

Goodbye, mane-overs.

Goodbye, Beak and his grape-eraser scent.

Goodbye, friends.

Goodbye, fun.

Goodbye, laughter.

Goodbye, family.

Goodbye, Charm House.

"You don't sound very happy."

"I don't feel very happy."

"Feelings aren't facts, you know," the Whisper said.

An invisible fist grabbed hold of Sadie's heart and squeezed. "Miss Flora used to say that, back when she was talking to me." She sighed. "But Miss Flora is wrong. In this case my feelings are a fact. I feel unhappy because I *am* unhappy."

"That will change."

Sadie rolled her eyes. What did this faceless know-it-all understand about feelings? It was nothing but a voice—a soft voice at that. "How will my unhappiness change?"

"You have to forgive yourself."

"For what? Losing my friends and failing my classes?"

"Grades are important. They reflect your drive, dedication, and priorities. And yes, you did lose sight of those things in pursuit of popularity. But grades aren't everything. Straight As may capture a teacher's attention, but character captures the heart. And you've shown tremendous heart."

"How? You wanted me to unite everyone and we're more divided than ever. Some lion-light I turned out to be."

"You're also part human."

"So?"

"You tripped over your pride."

Sadie thought of a lioness falling all over her cubs but couldn't bring herself to smile. Her goodbye visit turned into a lecture, another opportunity for someone to shine a light on her flaws.

"You think you can do everything alone, Sadie, and you can't. No great leader can."

Tears gathered behind Sadie's eyes. "What was I supposed to do? If I told Miss Flora that Lindsey stopped taking her elixir, I'd betray Lindsey. If I told Lindsey about her family, I'd betray Miss Flora."

"I don't blame you," the Whisper said. "I blame Miss Flora for putting you in that position."

"You do?" Sadie asked. It was the first time anyone showed compassion for the impossible situation she had been in.

"I do."

Sadie dried her cheeks on the sleeve of her sweatshirt. "Yeah, well, try telling her that."

The Whisper paused for a moment. "I don't have to."

"Why?"

"She already knows."

This time it was Sadie who paused. "How?"

"You just told her." The flames got bigger. "And she's very sorry for putting you in the middle of her family drama."

"Miss Flora?" Sadie stood and looked around the Den. "Is that *you*?"

"I told you, there's always a bigger cat. And believe it or not, this one has your back."

That's why the Whisper wasn't there on Monday. The Whisper was Miss Flora and Miss Flora had been gone.

"Keep your pride in check and your priorities straight and we'll turn you into the leader I know you can be."

That invisible fist came back for one more squeeze. "Actually, I have something to tell you."

The flames got even higher. The Den became warmer. Sadie was starting to sweat.

"My mom is picking me up tomorrow. I'm going home."

"No, you're not," Miss Flora said. "After you called her, she contacted me to find out what was going on. I assured her you were just nervous before a big test. Then I advised her to let you stay at Charm House because you have been working tirelessly to get your grades up and will continue to do so. Is that all right with you?"

Sadie leapt into the air. "Yes!" Her muscles overshot, and she banged her head on the ceiling of the cave, but she didn't care. This cat was getting another life.

"Now hurry up and get your cloak. We have a mandatory assembly to attend."

"Wait," Sadie pressed. "Where were you? Is Lindsey okay? Is she mad at you for not telling her about her family? Is Beak back? And what about—"

"Your cloak, Miss Samson."

"Right."

The cave door barely slid open before Sadie was out the door and racing toward her dorm room, her bed, her cloak, her home.

Hello, smokeless fire.

Hello, first tree.

Hello, fellow animal-lights.

Hello, dances in the clearing.

Hello, Paws, Claws, and Jaws.

Hello, mane-overs.

Hello, Beak and his grape-eraser scent.
Hello, friends.
Hello, fun.
Hello, laughter.
Hello, family.
Hello, Charm House.

twenty

Sadie was still sticking her arm through the sleeve of her cloak when she entered the barn. And yet, somehow Miss Flora was already on the throne, waiting for the nervous chatter to stop so she could begin.

How had the headmistress gotten there so quickly? Yes, she was a lion-light, but she was also, like, one hundred times older than Sadie. Why wasn't she panting or sweating or smoothing a disheveled cloak? How did her silver bob stay so strict and orderly? Sadie was beginning to think that Miss Flora was full of secrets, and not just the Lindsey kind.

"Good afternoon, lights," she finally said.

Everyone stood. "Good afternoon, Miss Flora," they sing-songed in unison.

The barn smelled like earth and oats, but there was something else too. Subtle. And sad. Like a grape-scented eraser that had been whittled down to a nub. Beak? Was he there? Or was this what missing him smelled like?

"Have a seat and remove your hoods," Miss Flora told them.

Sadie quickly claimed an empty hay bale by the door. Amy and Taylor were a few rows ahead and had no idea she was there. No one did. Which was beyond fine. Amy and Miss Flora might have forgiven her but there were dozens of girls who blamed her for Lindsey's absence. The closer she was to the exit, the better.

"As you know," Miss Flora continued, "Professor Jo and I were away this week. And so was Lindsey . . ."

Sadie searched the rows in front of her but couldn't find a single head with butterscotch-blond locks and zigzag stripes. Was Lindsey even there?

"Mark Twain once said, 'A lie can travel halfway around the world while the truth is putting on its shoes.' And, from what I understand, your lies have been on quite an adventure. All of the rumors you girls spread about who was responsible for our absence, why we left, and where we were . . . they stop now! It's time to give the truth a chance to speak." She looked to the hay bale on her left and nodded sharply. "Here to speak that truth is Miss Van der Beak."

What started out as a round of snaps for Miss Flora's guest speaker ended in a cacophony of gasps and chatter as the cloaked girl approached the throne. Shoulders back with her chin held high, her stride was strong and assured, but also graceful. Her emerald eyes, unmistakably fierce.

Lindsey!

She was as gorgeous as ever, but almost unrecognizable.

Her wild hair had been tamed into a quiet shade of blond and her open cloak revealed a white blouse neatly tucked into dark-wash jeans. No one knew that Lindsey's last name was really Van der Beak, not Striker, but when she held her unmanicured hands together in gratitude, the clang of gold bangles gave her away.

"Thank you, fellow lights . . . ," she said softly. She reached for her nail-file necklace, only to remember that it was gone. Just like her tight clothes, wedge sandals, and ride-or-die attitude. Yes, Lindsey was standing at the podium, but she too was gone. "And thank you, Miss Flora." She swatted herself on the side of her head and said, "I mean, *Grandma* Flora."

Chatter swelled among the girls, but Lindsey kept going.

"I know the truth about my family now, and you should, too. Miss Flora is my grandmother, Professor Jo is my mother, and I have a brother at Allendale. His name is Brett Van der Beak, aka Beak."

Sadie felt a zing inside her belly at the mention of his name. She missed him terribly, longed for the weight of his ring around her thumb. She felt untethered without it.

"They had to keep this secret from me—from everyone—to make sure I stayed at Charm House where I'd be safe. Every choice they made and everything they did was for my own good. I understand that now, and I forgive them. I forgive everyone."

Did Lindsey just glance at Sadie? Was Sadie *everyone*? It was hard to tell. The spark behind Lindsey's green eyes had smoldered and died.

"My rebellious stage is over," Lindsey said. "No more sneaking out. No more impulsive behavior. No more risks. I don't want to stand out anymore. I want to fit in . . ."

Sadie cocked her head. *Really?*

". . . We all have different animal-lights, but we need to come together as one species. We need to protect one another from IBS! Control our instincts! Blend in and stay safe!"

While the girls snapped their fingers and hissed with approval, Sadie wondered if this whole scene was a stress hallucination. Yes, this girl resembled Lindsey, but she didn't *sound* like Lindsey. She remembered that saying about ducks: If it looks like a duck, sounds like a duck, and acts like a duck, then it's a duck. But what if it only sort of looks like a tiger-light, barely sounds like a tiger-light, and is certainly not acting like a tiger-light? What then?

"This week," Lindsey continued, "my mother and grandmother took me to IBS . . ."

The barn started to smell like sardines and chocolate. *Fear.*

"Turns out my dad is Karl Van der Beak, a Typical who is also the medical director of IBS. He has no idea I'm a light but don't worry. I controlled my instincts and acted like I was there to visit. Professor Jo—I mean, my mom—taught me well, but make no mistake: He is the enemy. He doesn't know about Charm House, and he never can, or we'll end up in cages. I saw that place firsthand. It was scary."

"What did it look like?" Liv shouted. She was sitting between Mia and Val. Sadie had never heard such fear in a hyena-light's voice.

"It's brown, hive-shaped, and looks like it's made of honeycomb. It's got lots of little windows, but they're tinted. It's impossible to see inside."

"Did you find Kate?" yelled Taylor.

"No. My dad said he was too busy for a tour, so we stayed in the lobby. I thought about sneaking off, but security was thick. You need special access cards to go everywhere, so . . ." She glanced at Miss Flora, who nodded for her to continue. "The best way to support Kate is to listen to our teachers and lie low." She shrugged. "That's all. Thank you."

The girls watched in silence as Lindsey, or whoever that was, returned to her hay bale. Her sudden transformation was creepy, but on the bright side, her new attitude *would* keep them safe.

"That concludes our assembly," Miss Flora announced with a satisfied grin. "There is a football game at Allendale tomorrow, which you are free to attend so long as you follow Lindsey's lead and behave like Typicals. Enjoy the rest of the weekend."

Sadie joined the procession to the exit, wondering if she

should go to the game. Would anyone want to go with her? How would Beak react if he saw her there? Would she burst into tears if he ignored her again? Then she felt a tap on her shoulder.

"You're here!" It was Amy. Her gray eyes were wide with possibility, just like the day they met.

Sadie shrugged. "Yeah. My plans kind of changed so . . ."

"You're not the only one," Taylor muttered. She was referring to Lindsey and her new persona. It was a topic that Sadie was eager to discuss, and she would. But first . . .

"I'm sorry, Taylor, but were you talking to *me*?"

Taylor's skin darkened to match the dim lighting of the barn. "You and Amy," she said, eyes shifting. "Why?"

Sadie stopped walking, not caring one bit that she was holding up the line. When a girl loses everything and survives, losing everything no longer scares her. Getting lost a second time does. "You haven't spoken to me all week. Now you like me again?"

"I always liked you—"

"Well, you have an evil way of showing it."

"I know. Sorry. I tend to disappear when things get uncomfortable." The edges of Taylor's body began to fade and blend into the background. Within seconds, she was impossible to see. "I was hurt that you didn't trust me enough to tell me what was going on. Then I was mad at myself for feeling hurt because you were just being loyal to Miss Flora. Then I was too embarrassed to apologize. Then I was ashamed that I was too embarrassed. Then I was—"

"Taylor!" Amy interrupted. "Wrap it up."

"Lindsey's speech made me realize how complicated this whole thing was. And I miss you," Taylor said. "So I'm sorry for being so mad at you. Like, really sorry. And I'm sorry for disappearing. I'm working on that. And I'm sorry for—"

Sadie placed a hand on her heart. "I forgive you."

Taylor began to reappear. When she was fully visible, Sadie pulled her in for a hug and Amy piled on.

"Keep moving!" Ali Crawford called. "This is a fire hazard."

"So is your—" Sadie stopped herself. The goal was to unite these girls, not divide them. Starting now. "Sorry, Ali." Then, "I'm sorry, everyone!" Technically, Sadie was apologizing for anything she'd ever done to anyone, but she was looking at Mia when she said it. "Like Lindsey said, the enemy isn't in here, it's out there. From now on, we're one species. One kingdom. Free to hang with whoever we want whenever we want."

Mia's full-moon face lit up and she began yipping for joy. Within seconds, everyone joined her.

"I didn't know about you and Amy," Sadie told Mia as they stepped out into the sunlight.

Mia looked down at her checkerboard slip-ons. "Yeah."

"I know it's none of my business, but I hope you give it another chance."

"Same," Amy said, appearing at their side.

"Yeah." Mia blushed. "Same."

Liv and Val didn't exactly run over and envelop them in a group hug, but they didn't give them a hard time either. They simply let them be. It was progress.

"Pack attack!!"

Sadie, Taylor, and Amy turned to find Lindsey running toward them, fingers bent into the shape of paws and claws.

Sadie could hardly contain her joy. Her friend was back! Before any of them could ask her why she was acting so un-Lindsey-like they hugged, bear-light style, and didn't let go.

The Pack was back together, and Lindsey was home! Yes, she was tame, and maybe a little bit boring, but considering the few weeks Sadie had just had, boring was a welcomed change.

twenty-one

The aluminum plank under Sadie's butt was as cold and uncomfortable as the Cougars fans. She didn't understand much about football, but she knew that 21 for Milton Prep and 0 for Allendale wasn't good. And that she wanted to step up onto her cold, uncomfortable bleacher and chuck her popcorn bucket at the Milton cheerleading squad and send them ra-ra-right back to wherever they'd come from. Not because she gave two punts about football, but because the guy wearing the #11 jersey wasn't returning her texts.

Sadie checked her phone again.

"He still hasn't texted you?" Lindsey asked, as if nothing had ever happened between them.

Sadie had tried apologizing dozens of times, hoping for some of that "closure" her mother was always talking about. But Lindsey wasn't one for apologies or sappy exchanges. She was sitting knee to knee with Sadie, talking about boys, and sharing her lip gloss. All was forgiven.

"He hates me," Sadie said.

"He doesn't hate you; he was hurt. He thought you betrayed him, which you kinda did, but he forgives you. I swear."

"Okay, then explain why—" Sadie was about to interrogate Lindsey again. Ask her for the ninth time why Beak was icing her out. But Lindsey's answer was always the same: *You need to focus on your grades,* and that freaked her out even more, so she dropped the whole thing. "Explain why we aren't winning, because I really wish we were."

It wasn't a total lie. Lindsey had painted everyone's fingernails blue and red, Taylor spray-colored their hair, and Amy painted their faces. The species joined together to support the Allendale Cougars and Sadie wanted to believe their team spirit motivated the players. But the score being what it was, Sadie felt more like a spaz who slammed into a preschooler's art project.

"Too bad Cackle was fired," Amy said, obviously feeling it, too. She pinched off a pink fluff of cotton candy, then handed the swirl to Mia. "I wish you still had a squad," she said. "I wish you guys hadn't messed with Gleesa."

"Well, which one is it?" Mia asked. "The former or the *ladder?*"

Everyone laughed, bringing some much-needed levity to the sad scene. Then a burst of applause came from the other side of the field.

"What happened?" Sadie asked, as if she cared more about the busted score than her broken heart.

"Milton Prep is three yards from another touchdown," Taylor explained.

"That's bad, right?"

"Two-four-six-eight, things are not looking great," Taylor said. She pointed at the players as they shuffled into position, heads down, feet dragging. "It's like they've given up."

"Why isn't Coach Sterling giving them a pep talk or whatever it is they do in the movies?" Sadie asked. "What kind of a leader just stands there, pacing on the sidelines while his team fails?"

Her question was rhetorical, but still. No one even *tried* to answer. Her friends just looked at her, as if somehow she should know. And she sort of did.

The Whisper taught her all about great leaders, how they lift people up and inspire them. It told her to figure out what motivates her and to go after it. It told her to put her pride aside and prioritize. In other words, if Sadie couldn't connect with Beak on the phone, maybe she could connect with him on the field. "I have an idea! My dad always said the best defense is a good offense."

"What does that mean?" Sondra asked.

"I'm not sure, but we *can* raise the players' spirits and inspire them."

"Yeah, still," Sondra said. "What does that mean?"

Sadie sprang up from her aluminum plank. "It means, Taylor, assemble the Flash Lights."

Taylor stood. "Really?"

"Yes," Sadie said. "Mia, Liv, Val—do you remember your Cackle routine?"

They exchanged a look.

"Mostly," Val said.

"Good enough. Go stand on the left side of the field. Flash Lights, go to the right. The rest of us will stay near the bleachers. And remember, act like a Typical. Don't do anything they wouldn't do."

Sadie tensed a little, expecting Lindsey to push back, like she always did. But she simply stood there, hands in the pockets of her sensible jeans. Ready to cooperate.

"You want us to just stand here?" Kara asked.

"No, I want you to make some noise. Get everyone cheering. Let the players know we haven't given up and neither should they. Come on!"

The girls followed Sadie down the concrete stairs and took their positions. They weren't dressed in matching skirts, and they didn't have peppy pom-poms like Milton Prep, but their faces, hair, and fingernails were wild and painted. They looked like a team. They were a team.

Sadie turned to the crowd, lifted her hands into the air, and slow clapped.

Clap.

Clap.

Clap.

The students, teachers, and parents in the stands looked at one another, confused. Was Sadie about to land on social media as the lone clapper at a football game?

"Let's go," Sadie urged her crew.

The girls joined in. Then the students, the teachers, the parents, even Coach Sterling . . .

The clapping got faster and faster, providing the perfect beat for Taylor to count down and launch the Flash Lights into their fast-paced routine. Flips. Pivots. Cartwheels. The energetic monkey-lights twirled backward as Aubrey perfected her solo, which she didn't get the chance to do on Family Day because of her injury.

At the other side of the field, Cackle yipped, popped, and locked while Amy used her super-flexible skeleton to do a series of impossible back bends. The players stood there, amazed! The crowd was on their feet. The scoreboard flashed the word "*Fan*-tastic!"

When the whistle blew, the Cougars took their positions, hooting and hollering.

For the next thirty minutes, the crowd cheered, the girls danced, and the players played. *Hard.*

"Touchdown!" everyone shouted as #11 spiked the ball.

Beak!

Sadie was so busy keeping the energy up in the crowd she didn't realize the game had ended and she double didn't realize that Allendale had won. The boys ran toward one another and hugged. The girls did the same.

"Who's the captain of this ragtag squad?" Coach Sterling asked a few minutes later.

All fingers pointed to Sadie.

Uh-oh.

"What's your name?"

"Uh, Sadie."

"I'd like to see all of you at the rest of our games."

"You would?"

He nodded.

"There are a lot of us," Sadie warned. "Is that okay?"

"The more the merrier," Coach Sterling said.

And Sadie wholeheartedly agreed.

"Let's get choreographing!" Taylor announced.

Amy giggled. "I don't think 'choreographing' is a real word."

"*Yet,*" Taylor bellowed. The chameleon was confident. And giddy. They all were. Was it the rush that came from working together? The promise of a future beyond the Charm

House gates? The crushes they were about to have on the Allendale football players? Whatever the reason, the girls raced back to the barn to start "choreographing."

"Meet you there!" Sadie called after them. She was lingering by the bleachers, searching the popcorn-pocked ground for something she didn't lose. But Beak didn't know that. From the field, it looked like Sadie had lost something, something other than him.

She wanted Beak to spot her, jog over, take off his helmet, and beam forgiveness from those green eyes of his. But when she lifted her head and casually side-eyed the field, everyone was gone.

Limbs heavy and heart crushed, Sadie began that long walk through the woods toward Charm House. Yes, she united the species, created a new squad, and proved she could lead. But her success felt like failure, anyway.

It was as if Beak had trampled all over her spirit with his football cleats, poking holes in her happiness and draining her joy.

Then, the sound of snapping twigs. Someone was behind her. About a half mile away. She stopped.

Listened.

Looked.

Sniffed.

Smiled.

"Beak!" Sadie called before she even saw him. She was too excited. She didn't care. Then she did. The paint on her face. The nubby nails. The frizzy mane. Why wasn't she flat-ironed, mascaraed, and manicured?

Sadie was about to put on her hood, but Beak came into view. She froze instead. Froze and flushed.

"Hey," he said. His tone was icy and flat. Like a soldier returning from battle, a man forever changed.

"Hey."

He was still wearing his uniform. Still sweaty. Still icy. "Nice hair."

Was he seriously making fun of her? "If you're here to criticize—"

"No, I mean it. I like when you look like this."

"Like what?"

He looked down at his cleats and shrugged. "Like you."

The holes in her trampled spirit closed and the dancing mist returned.

Silence, as thick as the North Pacific fog, rolled in and settled between them. Sadie wanted to ask why he was holding a grudge, if he would ever friend her again on Trkr, and why Lindsey was acting so strange, but she didn't dare. Beak followed *her* into the woods. He would have to speak first.

"So, things got pretty weird between us, huh," he finally said.

Sadie pursed her lips and nodded.

"Sorry."

"For what?" She wasn't going to make this easy.

"For blocking you on Trkr."

Sadie laughed. "That's *it*?"

"And not returning your texts."

She folded her arms across her chest.

"And calls."

A crow cawed from a tree branch overhead. Beak, welcoming the distraction, squinted against the midday glare and watched the bird as if it were the most captivating creature ever. It was not.

"So is everything good now?" Sadie tried. She really wanted to ask if she could wear his thumb ring again but decided to play it cool.

"Well, my dad sucks, so there's that."

"No, I mean, are *we* good?"

"I forgive you and everything, so yeah. But—"

Panic smacked. "But what?"

"I think it's better if we're just friends."

The spirit holes returned, and the dancing mist evaporated. "Why?"

"I get that you were under a lot of pressure, but you promised you wouldn't tell and—"

"Beak, I didn't have a choice!"

"There's always a choice," said a girl.

Lindsey?

"Hey." She emerged from behind the tree. The crow flapped off with a final caw.

Sadie opened her mouth to explain herself (*again!*); as always, Lindsey beat her to it.

"You were asked to keep my grandmother's secret. You *chose* to tell our friends and protect me instead. You *chose* to fail Scent Ident to look for me. So yeah, there's always a choice."

"Okaaay."

"And now you have another choice to make."

Sadie looked to Beak for clarification. He met her gaze and nodded. *What was happening?*

Lindsey stepped closer and lowered her voice. "Beak and I are going to sneak into IBS and free the lights."

"What are you talking about?" Sadie said, confused. "You got up in front of the whole school and said—"

"Forget what I said. It's what I *do* that matters." Lindsey pulled a plastic card out of her back pocket. "I stole an access key from a security guard at IBS. And I memorized the building's floor plan off a blueprint on his desk."

"Seriously?" Sadie laughed uncomfortably. "You did?"

"When the venom finally left my system, I got my brain back."

"She has a photographic memory," Beak explained.

181

"I just forgot about it. Ha!" Lindsey reached into her blouse and pulled out her hidden nail-file necklace. "So, what do you say?"

"About what?" Sadie asked.

"Coming with us."

"To IBS?"

Lindsey nodded.

Sadie looked at Beak.

"What our dad is doing . . . ," he said. "It's wrong. He should be behind bars, not you guys."

"Yeah, but what are you going to do?"

"We were hoping you could help us figure that out," Beak said.

Sadie wanted to lead the lights to freedom, but was she ready to risk her life to do it? The Whisper said that great leaders unite people with a common goal. And the lights do want to be free. They also want to be in a cheerleading squad. Couldn't that be enough?

If Sadie wanted to be a real leader, the kind that changed the future and paved the way for others, this was her chance.

"What do Taylor and Amy think?"

"They don't know. They *can't* know," Lindsey insisted. "Cats only."

More lying?

"You saw what we did during the football game," Sadie pleaded. "When we work together, we can—"

"I said no." Her tone was fierce and final.

Sadie felt unsteady. Wasn't she the lion? The leader? The alpha? Or was Lindsey in charge now that she'd gotten her memory back? Her mission, her rules?

Sadie shook off her petty thoughts, held up her hand, and bent her fingers. "Paws and Claws," she said, giving in.

"Paws and Claws," Lindsey repeated.

"What about Paws, Claws, and Bruhs." Beak smiled.

Ahhh, that smile. Sadie missed it. She missed Beak. She missed Lindsey's fire. But she wouldn't have to. Not if she joined them.

"Okay," she said. "Let's do this!"

Acknowledgments

Hello, packmates. Here we are again.

As always, I have a long list of people to thank for helping me get this story into your hot little hands (or ears), starting with YOU.

Thank you, readers (and listeners), for allowing me to take you on another adventure. I'm tempted to bust out that old cliché and say I couldn't have done this without you. But I loathe clichés, and well, technically, I could have. It just wouldn't have been any fun.

Clichés aside, I *really* couldn't have published *Claw and Order* without the following people:

Kelsey Horton, my editor. Barbara Marcus, president of Random House Children's Books. Beverly Horowitz, publisher of Delacorte Press. Carol Ly and team, cover designers. Catherine O'Mara and team, marketing. Barbara Bakowski and Carrie Andrews, copyediting. Richard Abate, lifelong agent. Martha Stevens, Richard's right hand, who shall not be messed with. James Gregorio, contract king. Dina Santorelli, my right and left hands. You are incredible.

I *could* have published *Claw and Order* without the following people but would have sold fewer copies. Thank you, Shaila Gottlieb (Mom: 5 copies), Ken Gottlieb (Dad: 1 copy), Denise Gottlieb (definitely bought Ken's copy for him; probably read it for him too), Carly Cooper and Jack "Two Loops" Cooper (1 copy that Jack probably never read), B.J. and Jen Gottlieb (yeah, no, probably didn't buy one), Luke and Jesse Harrison (I gave them free copies, which they never read, so scratch them), Wyatt Peabody (1–5 copies—obligatory), Heaton Peabody (will probably gift one of his dad's copies to a cute sixth-grade girl).

Wow, that was depressing. I'm going back into book world, where people do what I say.

XOXO Lisi

About the Author

LISI HARRISON worked at MTV Networks in New York City for twelve years. She left her position as senior director of development in 2003 to write the Clique series, which sold more than eight million copies and remained on the *New York Times* bestseller list for more than two hundred weeks, with ten titles hitting #1 and foreign rights sold in thirty-three countries. *The Alphas* was a #1 *New York Times* bestseller, and *Monster High* was an instant bestseller. Her latest series are Girl Stuff and The Pack. Lisi lives in Laguna Beach, California.

LISIHARRISON.COM